CAPTAIN MANSANA,
AND OTHER STORIES.

CAPTAIN MANSANA,
AND OTHER STORIES.

BY

BJÖRNSTJERNE BJÖRNSON.

TRANSLATED FROM THE NORSE

BY

RASMUS B. ANDERSON.

AUTHOR'S EDITION.

Short Story Index Reprint Series

 BOOKS FOR LIBRARIES PRESS
FREEPORT, NEW YORK

First Published 1882
Reprinted 1969

STANDARD BOOK NUMBER:
8369-3236-6

LIBRARY OF CONGRESS CATALOG CARD NUMBER:
79-103494

PRINTED IN THE UNITED STATES OF AMERICA

PREFACE.

----◆----

"CAPTAIN MANSANA" is now presented for the
first time in an English dress. It was written, we
believe, shortly after Björnson's visit to Italy in 1872
and 1873. His own introductory letter is a sufficient
explanation of the character of the story. "The
Railroad and the Churchyard" was written many
years ago, and is found in the Copenhagen edition of
his collected stories. "Dust" is new, having been
published for the first time this year (1882) in the
January-February number of *Nyt Tidsskrift*, a new
magazine in Norway. All of Björnson's short stories have now been given in this edition of his works,
and of his long stories there remains only one,
"Magnhild," which will follow this volume and close
the series.

By the time this volume reaches the hands of the
reading public, Björnstjerne Björnson, and the three
Scandinavian countries with him, will have celebrated the twenty-fifth anniversary since the ap-

pearance of "Synnöve Solbakken" on the 10th of August, 1857. The novelist is twenty-five, the man will be fifty years old next December. Surely we on this side of the great ocean, too, congratulate him in our hearts and wish him a long life of happiness and prosperity.

RASMUS B. ANDERSON.

ASGARD, MADISON, WISCONSIN,
  August, 1882.

CONTENTS.

———◆———

INTRODUCTION TO CAPTAIN MANSANA.

THE following story appeared some years ago in a
Danish Christmas Gift, " Fra Fjæld og Dal " (From
Mountain and Valley), collected by Hr. H. J. Green-
steen.   In German the work has already passed
through two editions, and many have requested that
it might be published in a separate volume in our
language also.

Certain comments in the criticism of the public
press of Denmark and Sweden lead me to make the
following explanations : The narrative is in all es-
sentials historic ; above all, the most novel of its in-
cidents are historic — some of them even to their
most minute details.   Captain Mansana is drawn
from life ; what he is said to have performed, he
really did perform, and the singular destiny ascribed
to him is historically his in all that has a determin-
ing influence on his psychological development.

What induced me to make this presentation of his
character may be found in a few lines of Theresa's
letter, which concludes this story.

Compare her testimony concerning Mansana with the delineation of the character of Lassalle, published at the same time by Dr. Georg Brandes in his "The Nineteenth Century," and you will observe that the most secret impelling forces of Lassalle's destiny — which Brandes has depicted with so masterly a hand — are the same as those which controlled Mansana. Lassalle's rich intellectual powers, strong individuality, and great activity are naturally of far higher interest ; but the character-phenomenon is the same, and it entertained me, in its day, that we should both have had our attention drawn to this at the same time.

BJÖRNSTJERNE BJÖRNSON.

CAPTAIN MANSANA.

CHAPTER I.

As I was stepping into a railway car at Bologna, on a journey to Rome, I bought some
daily papers. Among these was a newspaper
from Florence, containing a letter from Rome,
that soon engrossed my undivided attention, for
it carried me back thirteen years to an earlier
visit to Rome and to my hosts in a little town
in the vicinity of the capital, which at that
time belonged to the Pope. The letter announced that the bones of the patriot Mansana,
who had been buried in the malefactors' grave-
yard at Rome, had now, in response to a petition from his native town, been disinterred, and
would, in the course of a few days, be received
by the authorities of that town, and attended
by delegates from various societies of Rome and
the adjacent towns to A——, Mansana's birthplace. A monument and solemn festal recep-

tion awaited them there; the martyr was to
have accorded him a tardy recompense.

Now I had lodged in this Mansana's house
thirteen years previous to this; his wife and
his younger brother's wife were my hostesses;
of the brothers themselves, the elder was a
captive in Rome, the younger an exile in Genoa.
' The letter, furthermore, depicted the career
of the elder Mansana. With the exception of
the last portion, I knew it before, and that was
just what increased my desire to join the procession which on the following Sunday was to
start from the Piazza Barberini in Rome and
end at A——.

And so on Sunday morning, at seven o'clock,
one gray October day, I found myself at the
appointed place. There were gathered together
a multiplicity of banners, accompanied by those
men, as a rule six, which each society had se-
lected for the purpose. My eyes were fixed on
a banner bearing the inscription, " The Struggle for the Fatherland," and to the accompany-
ing forms, in red shirts, with sashes about their
waists, cloaks thrown over their shoulders, pan-
taloons thrust into their boot-tops, and broad
hats, with floating plumes. What countenances! What wills! Those who have seen
the usual portrait of Orsini — he who threw

bombs at Napoleon the Third — well know the
Italian type of countenance belonging to the
men who rose in their might against the tyranny
of state and church, defying prisons and places
of execution, banding together in formidable
associations, progenitors of the army that freed
Italy.   Napoleon had been a member of such
a society.   He, as well as the rest of his comrades, had sworn that he would use whatever
position he might attain for Italy's unity and
welfare, or, in the opposite case, would forfeit
his life.   Now when Napoleon became Emperor
of France, it was the Carbonari comrade Orsini
who reminded him of his oath.   It was done in
such a way, too, that Napoleon knew what he
had to expect if he failed to keep it.

The impression Orsini's portrait made on me
the first time I saw it was that ten thousand
such men might conquer the world.   And here
I was in the presence of some of these men who
were endowed by the same public need with the
same will.   There had fallen a certain repose
over the wills now; but something dark about
the eyes told that it was not that of peace.
The medals on their breasts showed that they
had been present at Porte San Pancrazio in 1849,
when Garibaldi twice repulsed superior num-
l ers of Frenchmen; in 1858, at Lake Guarda;

and in 1859, in Sicily and at Naples. And what
the medals did not relate, also belonged, in all
likelihood, to the history of their lives, namely,
that they had fought at Mentana. It is just
such battle-fields as the latter, unrecognized by
the government, that are most deeply branded
into the souls of the people.   Napoleon was
made to feel this after he had secured the aid
of Italy against Germany ; it was Mentana that
forbade the king and the government to redeem
their pledge : to have done so would have cost
a crown.

The contrast between the dark, appalling
will of the Italian people and their mocking
levity or absolute indifference, is quite as great
as the contrast between these men of Orsini-
like will whom I here saw and the frivolous
countenances, expressing either refined scorn
or total apathy, among the surrounding spectators, as well as among the representatives who
accompanied the banners, bearing such inscriptions as " The Press," " Free Thought," " Free
Labor," etc., etc. Involuntarily I thought : it
is the levity of one half that forces the will of
the other half.   So great, so universal, had
been this levity, that great in proportion, dark
in proportion must be the will when roused.
And there ran through my mind the history of

Italy in her reckless frivolity and in the decrees
of her will.   I passed back and forth from Bru-
tus to Orsini, from Catilina to Cesare Borgia,
from Lucullus to Leo the Tenth, from Savo-
narola to Garibaldi, while the multitude was set
in motion, banners floated, heralds proclaimed
aloud the history of Mansana from the pages
and small pamphlets they held in their hands,
and the cortège turned into Via Felice.   Silence reigned : the lofty houses had but few spectators thus early in the morning, still fewer
when the procession wound its way into Via
Venti-Settembre, past the Quirinal; but the
numbers increased as it descended to the Foro
Romano and moved past the Coliseum to the
Porta Giovanni.   Outside of this the hearse
waited.   It had been provided by the municipal authorities ; servants of the law drove it.
Without delay it set forth.   Behind the hearse
walked two young men, one in civilian's dress,
the other wearing the uniform of a Bersaglieri
officer.   Both were tall, spare, muscular, with
small heads and low brows ; both alike in form
and in face, and yet so infinitely different.
They were the sons of the deceased.

I remembered them as boys of thirteen or
fourteen, and the circumstance to which my
recollections of them clung was curious enough ;

I remembered their father's aged mother throwing stones after them, and the boys standing at a distance laughing derisively at her. Suddenly I recalled with the utmost distinctness her strong, wrathful eye, her sinewy, but wrinkled hands. I could see her gray hair, bristling about the coffee-colored face ; and now as I looked at these boys I could almost have said that the stones she threw had not missed their mark and had become a part of them.

How their grandmother hated them ! Had they given her special cause for this ? That they had ; for hate begets hate, and war war. But at the outset ? Yes ; I was not with them at the time ; but it is not difficult to divine.

She had been early left a widow, this old woman, and in her strong, young beauty she turned the good graces and sympathy of the people into a source of income for herself and her two sons, one of whom now lay in the coffin ; the only beings she loved, and that with so "furious" a love that it wearied her sons. When they saw the wiles she employed in availing herself of her privileges as a pretty widow, to obtain benefits for her boys, they despised these benefits also. Once turned from her, they cast their affections on ideal things, such as Italy's freedom, Italy's unity, just as they had been taught by ardent young comrades: their mother's " frenzied " limitations in regard to what was her own, made them daily more enthusiastic to sacrifice everything for the common good. They were not merely as strong as she : they were stronger.

There arose sharp struggles in which she succumbed ; yet not entirely before their connections with secret societies had procured for them associations which extended far beyond their native town and the social circle to which her family belonged. Moreover, they each brought home a bride from a more distinguished house than their mother's, with an outfit larger than hers had been, and with a dower which she could not but call handsome. Then she was silenced for a time ; it seemed to her that, after all, this being a patriot was not without its advantages.

But the time came when both sons had to flee ; when the elder one was captured and cast into prison ; when the most monstrous public extortions began ; when unjust officials singled out defenseless widows as their prey. The time came when their house had to be mortgaged ; then their first vineyard ; finally their second. Aye, the time came when the first vineyard was seized by the mortgage holder !

And the time came when the two aristocratic wives, who had been friends from childhood, went out to service in the field, in the vineyard, and in houses ; when they had to take lodgers and wait upon them ; and for all this they were rewarded with words of derision, — not only by the clerical party, who under the papal dominion were the absolute rulers of the city, but by others ; for *they* were in the minority who honored wives for the sacrifices their husbands had made, and who united with them in hoping for freedom, enlightenment, and justice. Now the old woman had won ! But how ? So that she wept over her rejected love, her despised counsel, her lost property ; and rising up she cursed the sons who had forsaken and ruined her, until a single glance — no word was ever spoken — from the eldest daughter-in-law drove her back again to the hearth where she was in the habit of sitting, and where she passed her time in idleness when such spells came over her. Before very long she would leave the house, and if she met her grandsons, beneath whose low brows she unluckily thought she saw the bright gleam she had first adored, then feared in her own sons, she would draw them passionately to her, warn them against the ways of their fathers, grossly abuse the rabble, who were un-

worthy of the sacrifice of a penny, to say nothing of that of welfare, family, freedom ; and
then she would curse her sons, the boys' fathers ; they were the noblest, but at the same
time the most ungrateful and most foolish sons
that ever mother in that town had given birth
to ! And the unhappy woman would shake the
boys from her, crying, —

"Do be more reasonable, you worthless
scamps ! Why, you are standing there laughing ! Be not like your stupid mothers in there,
for they doted on the folly of my boys, — verily,
I am surrounded by lunatics ! "

And she would push her grandsons away and
weep, draw herself up, and then retreat. In
after years neither she nor the boys used much
ceremony in their dealings with one another.
They laughed at her when she had one of her
attacks, and *she* flung stones at them ; and at
last matters came to such a pass that if she
merely chanced to be sitting alone, the boys
would say, " Grandmother, have you gone mad
again ? " and then the stones would fly.

But why did not the old woman dare speak
in the presence of her daughter-in-law ? For
the same reason that she yielded in the presence of her sons in days of yore. Her husband
had been a sickly man, in no condition to man-

age his property; he had chosen her as the
complement of himself. To be sure, she raised
the property but she lowered him. *He* had a
refined smile, varied culture, and lofty aspira-
tions, and he suffered in her society. His nobler nature she could not destroy, — only his
peace of mind and his health. And so it happened that the beauty of character she had despised while he lived, gained the ascendency
over her after his death. And when it reap-
peared as an inspiration in her sons, and as a
reproachful reminder in the pure eyes of her
daughter-in-law, she was conquered completely.

I say the grandmother's stones had not missed
their mark, and were lodged in her grandsons.
Look at those two men marching there! The
youngest, the one in civilian's dress, had a
smile about his rather thin lips, a smile, too, in
his small eyes; but I do not believe it would
have been well to irritate him. He had been
helped on in the world by his father's political
friends, had early learned to bow and offer
thanks, — I think not, however, through gratitude.

But look at the elder! The same small head,
the same low brow, yet both broader. No
smile about either lips or eyes. I did not even
wish to see him smile. Tall and slim like his

brother, he was even more bony; and while both men gave the impression of gymnastic strength, and looked as if they were quite able to leap over the hearse, the elder one gave the additional impression of literally desiring to do so; for the half lounging gait of the brothers, the evident result of unused powers, had become in the elder an impatient elasticity, — he seemed to walk on springs. His thoughts were apparently absent, for his eyes wandered far beyond all surrounding objects; and when later I offered him my card and reminded him of our former acquaintance, I had proof that this was really the case.

I conversed with several persons in the procession who were from the patriot's town. I inquired after grandmother Mansana. There was a general smile, and several at the same time eagerly told me that she had lived until the previous year: she had reached the age of ninety-five. I perceived that she was understood. It was told me with equal zeal that before her death she had experienced the satisfaction of seeing her home fully her own again: the one vineyard had been repurchased, and both were free from debt, as were also the fields. All was done out of gratitude to the patriot martyr, whose glory was now on all lips;

it had become the pride of the town ; his life, and that of his brother were, in fact, its sole contribution to the work of deliverance.

So she had lived to see all *this !*

And I inquired after the wives of the two martyrs, and learned that the younger one had succumbed under her calamities, especially her grief at the loss of her only daughter. But the wife of the elder Mansana, the mother of the two young men, was living. The faces of the narrators became grave, their voices hushed, the conversation was ere long conducted by one individual, with occasional additional remarks by the others, all with a certain slow solemnity. She had evidently acquired power over them, this pure woman, with her grand soul. I heard how she had put herself in communication with her husband while he was yet in prison, had informed him that Garibaldi had instigated a revolt within the town and an attack from without, and that the people were waiting for Mansana to be free ; he was to be the leader of the work in Rome. And he became free ! He owed this to his own rare strength of will and to his wife's wise fidelity. He feigned insanity, that was her counsel; he shrieked until his voice was gone, then until his strength was exhausted; for in the mean time he had not taken a mouthful either of food or of drink. Almost at death's door, he persevered in this course, until he was transferred to an insane hospital. His wife could visit him there, and from there they fled — not out of the city ; no, the great preparations demanded his presence, and she first waited upon him, afterwards shared his hazardous undertaking. Who else in his place, after so long an imprisonment, would not have sought freedom's soil, when it was but two or three miles distant? But one of those for whom he risked life and all that was his, betrayed him ; he was again taken captive, and without him a large part of the plan became fruitless : that is to say, it resulted in defeat on the frontiers ; in the conviction, imprisonment or death of thousands in the capital and in the provinces. Before the clock struck the hour of freedom, he had been beheaded and buried amongst his dead fellow-prisoners, thieves and murderers, in the great malefactors' burying ground of the capital — from which to-day his bones had been disinterred.

Now the widow, enveloped in a long black veil, stood waiting for him at the head of the multitude in the flag-adorned church-yard of his native town, beside the already completed monument. That same day, after the new burial, it was to be unveiled amid the thunder of cannon, to which a festal illumination on the mountains, later in the evening, was to give response.

Our way led over the yellow gray Campagna up towards the mountains ; we advanced from one mountain town to another, and everywhere there extended, as far as the eye could reach, a human throng, with uncovered heads. The peasantry from the neighboring towns had assembled in haste ; choruses of music rang through the narrow streets, streamers and flags hung from every window, garlands fell, flowers were strewed about, handkerchiefs waved, and tears glistened. We soon arrived at Mansana's native town, where the reception was still more affecting, and whither no insignificant portion of the large masses from the other towns had followed us. But the crowd was greatest at the church-yard.

I, however, as a stranger, was favored, and had assigned to me a place not far from the widow. Many wept at sight of her, but she kept her quiet gaze fixed unmovedly on the coffin, the flowers, the multitude. *She* did not weep ; for the whole of this combined could not restore to her him whom she had lost, nor did it invest him with increased honor in her eyes.

She looked upon it all as upon something that had been known to her for years before this day. How beautiful she was! By this remark I do not mean to refer only to the noble lines which could never be wholly obliterated in a face or in eyes which had once been the most beautiful in the town, indeed were still so when I saw her thirteen years before this, although even then she showed traces of having wept too much. No, I refer also to the actual halo of truth that surrounded her form, movements, countenance, gaze. It made itself manifest in the same way as the light, and like this it transfigured whatever it fell upon.

I shall never forget the meeting between her and her sons. They both embraced and kissed her; she held them each in turn long in her arms, as though she were praying over them. A hush fell over all, some involuntarily removed their hats. The younger son, whom she first embraced, drew back, with his handkerchief to his eyes. The elder stood still, for she looked at him — aye, looked at him; *every* eye was turned on him, and he colored deeply. There was unspeakable pain in that look, an unfathomable prophecy. How often I have since recalled it! With his face dyed crimson, he firmly returned her gaze, and she looked

away that she might not goad him to defiance.
It was quite apparent that this was so. The
tendencies of the two families stood face to
face.

CHAPTER II.

On the way back, it was not the touching
revelation of the mother that was most prom-
inent in all I had experienced, it was the Bersaglieri officer's defiant countenance, his tall,
bony form, and athletic bearing. And thus it
was that I could not help inquiring about him.
To my surprise, I found that it was the daring
exploits of this son that had again drawn attention to the father, and called forth the honor
so late accorded to his memory. I had fallen
upon something genuinely Italian. Concerning
father, mother, speeches, reception, beauties of
scenery surrounding the last solemnities at the
church-yard, torchlights in the mountains, —
of all these things not a word was spoken !
Until we parted in Rome, we were entertained
with anecdotes about the Bersaglieri officer.

When yet a boy he had been with Garibaldi,
and had won favor to such a degree that later

he was kept at a military school by his own and his father's friends.

A command was intrusted to him, as to so many Italians in those days, before the final examination was passed, and soon he had so distinguished himself that he received a permanent appointment. One solitary deed bore his name over Italy, even before he had been in a battle. He was one of a reconnoitring party; and having wound his way by chance and alone up to the top of a wooded height, he espied, in a thicket behind it, a horse, soon another, drew nearer, saw a traveling carriage, came still closer, and discovered a group of people, a lady and two servants encamped in the grass. He promptly recognized them. The lady had the previous day come driving toward the vanguard, seeking refuge from the enemy, of whom she declared herself afraid. She had been allowed to pass; and now she had returned by another route, and she and her servants were seeking repose in this spot. The horses had an ill-used look; they had been driven the whole night, and that so hard that it was impossible to progress without first having some rest. All this Mansana read, as it were, at a glance.

It was on a Sunday morning; the Italian troops were in camp; mass had just been read,

and they were at breakfast when the outposts
saw young Mansana coming galloping toward
them with a lady on the pommel of his saddle
and two unharnessed horses fastened to the latter.   The lady was a spy from the enemy's
army ; her "two servants," officers of the hos-
tile force, lay wounded in the woods.   The lady
was recognized at once, and Mansana's "Evviva!" reëchoed by thousands.   The troops
broke up; the enemy must be near at hand, and
it was soon ascertained that this Giuseppe Mansana's presence of mind had saved the vanguard
from falling into a snare.

I shall tell many anecdotes about him ; but
in order that they may be understood, I must
begin by stating that he was the first gymnast
and fencer in the army.   Both now and later I
heard but one opinion of this.

Immediately after the war he was in garrison
at Florence.   One day it was told at an officers'
café that a Belgian officer, who a few weeks before had been stationed there, had proved to
be in reality a papal officer, and now amused
himself among his comrades in Rome by making sport of the Italian officers, whom, with a
few exceptions, he pronounced mere ignorant
parade puppets, whose main characteristic was
childish vanity.   This story excited much in-

dignation among the officers of the garrison in
Florence, and from the café where he had heard
it young Mansana went at once to the colonel
and asked for a six days'· furlough. This was
granted him. He went home, purchased civilian's clothes, and without delay took the direct
route to Rome. By the way of the forest he
crossed the frontier, and on the third day appeared in the officers' café in Rome, near the
Piazza Colonna, where he soon saw sitting before him the Belgian papal officer. He walked
up to the latter and quietly bade him follow
him outside. Here Mansana told the officer
who he was, bade him take a friend and accompany him beyond the gates, to give satisfaction to the Italian corps of officers in a duel
with him. So frankly and completely did Man-
sana· trust to the honor of this man that the
latter could not fail him. He immediately went
in after a friend, and three hours later was a
corpse. But young Mansana set out forthwith
on his return route through the forest to Florence. Not by him was the affair made known
in Florence, where, meanwhile, he had remained, but through tidings from Rome, and
he was sentenced to a long imprisonment for
having left the town without permission and
for having furthermore been in another coun-

try; but the officers made a banquet for him when he was free and the king honored him with a decoration.

Shortly afterward he was stationed at a Salerno garrison. Smuggling had become rife on the coast, and the troops were aiding in putting a stop to it. In civilian's dress he went out to make observations, and learned at an inn that a ship carrying smuggled goods was now lying out beyond the range of vision, and was to near the coast under the cover of night. He went home, changed his clothes, took with him two chosen men, and toward evening they all three rowed out in a frail little boat. I heard this anecdote told and confirmed on the spot. I have heard it since from others; and later had the opportunity of reading it in the newspapers; but nevertheless it always remains incomprehensible to me, how in boarding a vessel with his two followers he could compel sixteen — sixteen — men to obedience, as he did, and bring the ship to the wharf!

After the capture of Rome, in which he also took part, and where he worked miracles, especially during the inundation which followed, he was sitting one evening in the same officers' café, in front of which he had challenged the Belgian papal officer. He there heard some brother officers who had just come from a social gathering, telling about a Hungarian who had drank too much Italian wine, and under its inspiring influence had fallen to boasting about the Hungarians, to such an extent that, after some slight opposition, he had even gone so far as to assert that three Italians would be welcome to attack one Hungarian! All the officers laughed with those who were telling this, all with the exception of Giuseppe Mansana.

"Where does this Hungarian lodge?" asked he.

His tone was one of utter indifference; he neither looked up nor removed the cigarette from his mouth. The Hungarian had been followed home, so the desired information was at once given. Mansana rose.

"Are you going?" asked they.

"To be sure," he replied.

"But surely not to the Hungarian?" some one inquired, good-naturedly.

Now there was nothing good-natured about Giuseppe Mansana.

"Where else?" cried he, and strode away.

The rest rose at once to accompany him. They endeavored on the way to make him sensible of the fact that a drunken man could not be called to account.

"Do not be alarmed," was Mansana's response, "I shall treat him accordingly."

The Hungarian lodged on the *primo piano*, as the Italians say, that is, on the second floor, of a large building in Fratina. In front of the windows of the first floor (*parterre*), in every Italian town, there are iron bars, and these Giuseppe Mansana grasped, swung himself up, and soon stood on the balcony outside of the Hungarian's chamber. He broke in the panes of the balcony window, opened it and disappeared. There was a light struck within — this his comrades who stood below saw. What else transpired they could not ascertain; they heard no noise, and Mansana has never told them. But after the lapse of a few minutes he and the Hungarian, the latter in his shirt, came out on the balcony, whereupon the Hungarian declared, in good French, that he had been drunk that evening, and begged pardon for what he had said; of course an Italian was just as good as a Hungarian. Mansana came down again the same way he had gone up.

Greater and lesser anecdotes from war times, from garrison and social life (among these some stories of racing which testified of an endurance in running I have never heard equaled), fell like hail upon us; but all that was told presents, it seems to me, the picture of a man whose presence of mind, courage, love of honor, whose physical strength and energy, dexterity and shrewdness, rouse to the highest pitch our expectations as to his future possibilities, but at the same time fill us with solicitude.

How Giuseppe Mansana came the following winter and spring to engross the attention of thousands, and among them the author of this volume, will appear in the story itself.

CHAPTER III.

WHEN Giuseppe Mansana followed his father's bones to their honored grave, looking as though he would like to leap over the hearse, he was — it soon became manifest — under the influence of a first passionate love. That same evening he took the railway train for Ancona, where his regiment was stationed. It was there she lived, the mere sight of whom had power to subdue the flames which burned with such consuming force.

He was in love with one who had his nature, one who must be conquered, one who had taken

3

captive hundreds without being herself captured, one of whom an enamored Ancona bard
had sung —

> Thou dusky devil, I do love thee,
> Thy smile of fire, thy blood of wine,
> And think it is the glow of evil
> Makes beauty in thy courage shine.
> Nay, think, the play which never ceases
> Of lustre in your face and eyes
> Is Satan's unrest in your nature,
> Your winning laughter his outvies.
> I think so, fair one ! — but much rather
> I thee would love 'mid death and tears,
> Than fall asleep in arms that carry
> Me to the grave for fifty years.
> Yea, rather, much the queen of living
> In majesty that ends no more,
> E'en though I sink before the riddle,
> Than follow what I know before.

She was the daughter of an Austrian general
and a lady who belonged to one of the oldest
families in Ancona. It caused much indignation in its day that a woman of her rank should
marry the commander of the detested foreign
garrison.

The indignation was, if possible, increased
by the fact that *he* was almost an old man,
while *she* was but eighteen years of age and
very beautiful. But the general's immense fortune might have tempted her; for she lived in
her splendid palace in actual poverty, — a
matter of common occurrence in Italy. The

fact is, the family palace is usually entailed property which the occupant is often unable to keep in repair. This was very nearly the case in the present instance. There might, however, have been some other attraction besides the general's wealth, for when, shortly after their daughter's birth, he died, the widow passed her period of mourning in absolute retirement. The church and the priest alone saw her. Friends, with whom she had broken at the time of her marriage, yet who now put themselves to all sorts of trouble in their efforts to again approach the enormously wealthy widow, she fled from.

Ancona, meanwhile, became Italian, and from the festivals, illuminations, and rejoicings she fled still farther, namely, to Rome, while her palace in Ancona, as well as her villa by the sea, remained closed and deserted as a mute protest. But in Rome, Princess Leaney discarded the black veil, without which no one had seen her since her husband's death, opened her salon, in which might be seen all the highest aristocracy of the papal dominion, and annually contributed large sums to the Peterpence fund and other papal objects. The first as well as the last increased the hatred felt for her in Ancona, and which through the liberal party was also transported to Rome; and even on Monte Pincio, when, in all her beauty and splendor, she drove out with her little daughter, she could detect it in the glances flashed on her by familiar faces from Ancona and unfamiliar ones from Rome. She defied it, and not only regularly made her appearance on Monte Pincio, but also repaired anew to Ancona when summer drove her away from Rome. Once more she opened her Ancona palace and her villa, and passed most of the time in the latter place in order to avail herself of the baths. She made a point of driving through the town to her house on the Corso or to the church without greeting any one or being greeted in return, but nevertheless she repeated the trip every day. When her daughter grew larger, she allowed her to take part in the evening entertainments of plays and tableaux, which the priests of the city, under the protection of the bishop, got up for the benefit of the Peter-pence fund in Ancona; and so great was the child's beauty and the mother's attractiveness that many attended who would not otherwise have been willing to go. Thus the daughter learned defiance of the mother; and when at fourteen years of age the young girl lost her mother, she persevered in it on her own account, and with such additions as youth and courage involuntarily supply.

She was soon more talked about and more severely censured than her mother had ever been, inasmuch as her renown was more widely spread. For with an older lady, whom she took as a companion, a dignified, elegant person, who saw everything but spoke of nothing, she roamed through other countries, from England to Egypt, so planning her journeys, however, that she always passed her summers in Ancona, her autumns in Rome.

The last-named city became Italian finally, as well as Ancona; but in both cities she continued to lead what might be called a challenging life in the face of those who *now* ruled, and who sought in every way to win the rich, handsome woman. Indeed, it has been asserted that young noblemen formed alliances to conquer or crush her. Be this true or not, she believed it herself. And so she lured into her presence those whom she suspected, only to repulse them mercilessly. She first made them mad with hope, then with disappointment. She drove her horses herself through the Corso and on Monte Pincio; she appeared as a victor on a triumphal progress, with those she had vanquished bound to her carriage; not every one, to be sure, could see this, but *she* saw it because she felt it, and her victims felt it too.

She would have been slain, or even worse, had she not had too many worshipers, who in spite of everything formed a body-guard of perpetual adoration about her. To these belonged the bard before mentioned.

Above all else she became the secret hope and the open hatred of the young officers of the Ancona garrison.

Just at the time when Giuseppe Mansana had been removed with his Bersagliers to Ancona, she had been exercising a new caprice in that place. She had resolutely refused to adorn the company that assembled of evenings on the Corso, in order to promenade up and down, by the light of the moon, stars, and gas, the ladies in ball costume, holding before their faces the fans they can use with such wondrous effect, the gentlemen swarming around in fine new summer suits, or in their uniforms, meeting friends and acquaintances, laughing, gathering together about tables, where groups were already seated enjoying ices and coffee, then passing from these to others, finally to drop down at one themselves, while a quartet, or a wandering chorus, with cithern, flute, and guitar might be heard — Theresa Leaney resolutely refused to contribute to the splendor, the curiosity, the enjoyment, the nobility of these daily exhibitions of the town; on the contrary, she had chosen to be the cause of disturbance.

At sunset, when the carriages of other wealthy people were returning home, she drove out. With two unusually small ponies, the " Corsicans," by name, which she had that summer purchased, and, as was her wont, herself holding the reins, she would drive through the town in full trot. Then when the Corso was lighted and the rendezvous had begun, — the general rendezvous between families and friends, the clandestine one between young maidens and their adorers, the silent one between the idler and his shadow, the sighing one between the far-off betrothed lover and his faithful damsel here present, the brief one between the officer and his creditor, the excessively courteous one between the official and him whose death will give him a higher post, — just as the young ladies had succeeded in twice displaying their new Parisian dresses, that is to say, in one promenade up and one down the street, and the admiring store clerks had passed through the preliminaries, and the officers had formed their first critical group, and the nobility had just condescended to notice attentions, — this arrogant young girl, with her rigid, elderly companion at her side, would come dashing full speed into the midst of the group. The two little ponies would be in full trot, and the officers and young ladies, the nobility and the store clerks, family groups and whispering couples, must part in the utmost haste, in order to escape being run over. A row of bells on the harness of the ponies gave due warning, it was true, so that the police could say nothing ; but all the more did those have to say whom she had insulted twofold: first by her absence, and then by her presence.

Two evenings Giuseppe Mansana had been on the Corso, and both times had come near being run over. He never before conceived the possibility of such assurance. He learned, too, who she was.

The third evening, when Theresa Leaney stopped at the accustomed place outside of the town, on her return trip, to have her ponies watered and allow them to rest before beginning their trot to the town and its Corso, a tall man stepped forward and saluted her. He was an officer.

" I take the liberty," said he, " of introducing myself. I am Giuseppe Mansana, officer of the Bersagliers. I have laid a wager to run a race

with your little ponies from here to town.
Have you any objections?"

It was after dusk, so that under ordinary
circumstances she would not have been able to
see him; but a strong excitement will sometimes increase our powers of vision. Astonishment, combined with a trifling degree of alarm
— for there was something in the voice and
bearing that startled her — gave her courage;
for we often become courageous through fear.
And so turning toward the small head and
short face, of which she caught a faint glimpse,
she said, —

" It occurs to me that a *gentleman* would have
asked my permission before entering into such
a wager; but an Italian officer " —

She did not continue, for she grew frightened
herself at what she was saying, and there
arose an ominous silence, during which her uneasiness increased. At last, she heard from a
voice whose tones were more hollow than
ever (Mansana's voice always had a hollow
sound), —

" The wager is entered into with myself
alone, and, to speak frankly, I propose to make
the attempt, whether you consent or not."

" What? " exclaimed she, seizing the reins;
but at the same moment she uttered a shriek

and her companion a still louder one, as both
came near falling from the carriage; for with
a long whip neither of them had until now
perceived the officer gave the ponies a furious
cut across the backs, so that with a plunge they
darted forward. Two servants, who had been
sitting behind, and who had started to their feet
at a sign from their young mistress to come
to her aid, were thrown to the ground. Neither
of them took part in the drive that now began,
and that was not so long as it was rich in in-
cidents.

To Giuseppe Mansana's acquirements — and
possibly it was the most practiced of these —
belonged, as indicated before, the art of running. The little ponies were not so hard to
keep pace with, especially at the outset, when
they were vigorously held back and were therefore not quite sure whether they should trot
or not. Theresa, in her wrath, was ready to
venture everything rather than tolerate such
humiliation. She was determined, therefore, to
give her servants time to catch up to her. But
just as she was about to succeed in bringing
the ponies to a halt, the lash fell whizzing on
their backs and forthwith they darted off again.
She said not a word, but drew in the reins
again, and that so persistently that the ponies

were about to halt once more; but then the
whip fell anew, and again and yet again. And
now she and they gave it up. Her elderly companion, who the whole time had shrieked and
clung with both arms to Princess Leaney's
waist, fell into a swoon, and had to be sup-
ported. Anger and dismay overwhelmed Theresa; for a while she saw neither ponies nor
road, and at last she did not so much as know
whether she held the reins. She had indeed
dropped them but found them again in her lap,
and made a second trial, holding her companion
with one arm, yet at the same time managing to
grasp the reins with both hands, striving with
all her might to gain control of the terrified
little ponies. She soon realized the impossibil-
ity of this. It was dark; the tall poplars
trotted with them in the air step by step, above
the brushwood that grew between them. She
knew not where she was. The sole object she
could distinguish besides the ponies was the tall
form by their side, that like a spectre towered
above them, always at the same height and the
same distance. Where were they going? And
swift as lightning it flashed through her mind:
"Not to the town; he is no officer, he is a
bandit; I am being driven away from the road
— soon others will 'oin him!" And from the

depths of the anguish caused by this sudden
idea, she screamed, —

"Stop, for Heaven's sake! What do you
want? Do you not see " —

She got no farther, for she heard a whizzing
sound in the air, the whip cracked on the backs
of the ponies, and harder than ever the little
animals dashed onward.

Swift as the speed of the ponies was the flight
of her thoughts. "What does he want? Who
is he? One of those whom I have insulted?"
And in rapid succession the ranks of these passed
in review before her. She could find no one
whom he seemed to resemble. But the thought
of vengeance pursued her startled conscience;
it might indeed be one whom she did not know,
but who wanted to take revenge for all the others. But if this was revenge, she had yet the
worst to expect. The bells cut through the rattling of the carriage-wheels; the short, sharp
sound darted about her like shrieks of anguish,
and, roused to the utmost by terror, she was
ready to risk a leap from the carriage. But no
sooner had she relaxed her hold on her companion than the latter rolled over like a lifeless object, and in greater terror than ever the princess
picked her up, and with the rigid form thrown
across her lap sat a long time devoid of a single

clear idea. At last, as the road made a sudden turn, she perceived a luminous haze over the town. She felt the joy of deliverance, but only for a moment, brief as a glance, for the next instant she comprehended the whole : he was an avenger from the Corso !

" Oh, no farther ! " exclaimed she, even before the thought was fully matured. " Oh, no ! "

The words echoed in her ears, the bells leaped with shrill intonation about the group, the poplars trotted alongside, but that was all : the race went on, but there came no answer. She saw in her mind's eye her pitiful progress through the city, lashed forward with her fainting companion in her arms, and the public on either side, with the officers foremost applauding and jeering. For this was the officers' revenge ; she was sure of it now. She bowed her head as if she were already there. Then she felt and heard that the ponies were slackening their speed ; they must be near their destination ; but would they pause before they got there ? Once more, with a sudden hope, she looked up. He had dropped behind, — that was the cause of this respite. He was close by her side ; soon she heard his hasty, labored breathing, heard finally nothing else, until all her anxiety became centred in the thought, " What if he should fall in the middle of the Corso, with blood streaming from his lips and nostrils ! " His blood would then be on her head ; for her challenging defiance had called forth his. The people would spring upon her and tear her to pieces.

" Spare yourself ! " she begged. " I will yield ! " she cried, in tones of agonized entreaty.

But as though startled out of his artful experiment, he made one final effort, and in two or three longer strides was once more abreast with the ponies, who the moment they became conscious of his presence, accelerated their speed, but received, nevertheless, two whizzing lash strokes.

Now she distinctly saw the first gas-lights near the Cavour monument ; soon they would turn into the Corso ; the play was about to begin. She felt an unconquerable desire to weep, and yet could not shed a tear, and then she bowed her head in order to shut out all further sight. At that moment she heard the sound of his voice, but not what he said ; the carriage was now on the paving-stones, and besides, he was most likely unable to speak distinctly. She looked up again, but he was no longer visible. Great God ! had he fallen to the ground ? Every drop of blood stood still within her veins. No: there he was, walking slowly away from the Corso, past the Café Garibaldi. At the same moment she found herself in the Corso; the horses trotted, the people cleared the way; she bowed her head still lower over the fainting companion lying across her lap; terror and shame were chasing after them with the lash.

When some moments later she came to a halt in the palace court-yard, through whose open gate the ponies had rushed full speed, so that it was a miracle the carriage was not upset or dashed to pieces, — she too fainted.

An old servant stood awaiting her coming. He called for help; the two ladies were borne into the palace. Shortly afterward the men who had been thrown from the carriage made their appearance, and related what had occurred, so far as they knew it. The old servant took them soundly to task for their awkwardness, so that they actually felt ashamed of it themselves, and all the more readily did as he bade them: maintained a discreet silence.

The ponies had run away just as the servants, after a short rest, were about mounting the box. That was all.

CHAPTER IV.

WHEN Princess Theresa Leaney awoke to consciousness her strength seemed wholly exhausted. She did not rise from her couch, she scarcely ate a morsel; no one was allowed to remain with her.

Her companion walked noiselessly through the great mirrored hall opposite the ante-room, and noiselessly back again when she had finished her errands. Just as noiselessly she stepped back into the small gothic chamber occupied by the princess. The servants followed her example. Princess Leaney's companion had been brought up in a convent, had come forth from there with high pretensions on the score of her rank and her acquirements, pretensions she maintained for ten years and then for five more — constantly outraged by the inelegance and greed of youth. Finally she obtained in an aristocratic family a position befitting a lady of rank, still silently preserving her feeling of injured dignity; but as she grew older she submitted to one thing after another, without, however, losing her sense of affront; she held her peace about everything and devoted all her energies to the accumulation of wealth. Her great secret of success lay in making herself thoroughly acquainted with all that concerned her lofty patrons, and in using her knowledge to the profit of *both* parties.

And so she was silent. After the lapse of a few days there came from the gothic chamber of the princess the curt little command : " Pack up ! " From later bulletins it was ascertained that a very long journey was in prospect. In a few days more the princess came forth herself, walked about slowly and silently, gave orders concerning some trifles and wrote some letters. After this she disappeared again. The next day brought the message : " This evening at seven o'clock." At the stroke of six she appeared herself in traveling costume, accompanied by her maid, who was also dressed for traveling. The companion stood ready for departure beside the trunks which the servant, who was all ready too, was to close, after the princess had cast an approving glance at their contents.

The first word the companion had spoken to Princess Leaney since their memorable drive she now uttered. As though by chance she placed herself at the side of the princess, and looking out into the court-yard softly observed:

4

" People in town only know that our ponies ran away — nothing more."

A withering look of displeasure met her gaze; this was gradually transformed into one of astonishment, and this in turn into one of dismay.

" Is he then dead ? " the princess gasped, and every word quivered with agonized dread.

" No, I saw him an hour since."

The companion did not return the look the princess gave her, nor had she done so before; she was gazing out into the court-yard toward the stable, from which the carriage had been drawn out and the horses just led forward. When finally she found it advisable to turn, — and it was long before she did find this advisable, as the princess said nothing and the servant did not stir ; he must have seen something before him which riveted him to the spot, — when finally the companion deemed it advisable to turn she saw in the twinkling of an eye that the effect of her information had been complete. The terrified imagination of the princess had naturally, during these feverish days, pictured the jubilant derision which must now fill the town ; she had fancied it spreading as far as Rome, indeed, through the newspapers, over the whole world ; she had felt her hitherto un-

bowed, brilliant defiance annihilated in a few
hideous moments; it had seemed to her as if
she had been dragged through the mire by the
hair of her head. And so no one besides him
and themselves knew what had occurred ? He
had kept perfectly silent ? What a man !

The beautiful large eyes of the princess
darted flashes of fire around the room, but
shortly afterward they assumed a laughing ra-
diance ; she drew up her head and her whole
figure, took several turns up and down the
room, as far as the trunks and other traveling
luggage permitted, then smiling and giving her
parasol a little twirl, she said, —

" Unpack ! We will not go to-day ! "

Then she abruptly left the room.

In a short time the maid came and asked the
companion to dress for a walk.

As often and as long as they had been in
Ancona it was the first time the princess had
been willing to take part in the evening promenade of the fashionable world. Therefore the
companion would have had opportunity for
some astonished words in reply to the look of
astonishment with which the maid accompanied
this announcement ; but the look was in itself
an impertinence, and so there was nothing
said. When Theresa, all dressed, entered the

great mirror-lined, pillared salon, she could see
through the open door into the faintly-lighted
ante-room, and there she beheld her companion
standing waiting. The costume of the princess
alone would have justified the maid's expression of countenance as she opened and closed the
door ; but the companion followed as though
they had been every day accustomed to make
this expedition and as though the princess appeared every evening in such elegant attire.

In a lilac silk dress, richly trimmed with
lace, she rustled down the steps. Her figure
was vigorous and already rather full, and yet it
gave an impression of suppleness because she
was also tall and had a certain vivacious bearing. Contrary to her custom she now wore her
hair dressed in braids, and there floated behind
her a long lace veil, fastened on one side of the
head with a brooch, on the other with a rose ;
the sleeves of her dress were so open that when
she used her fan, her long gloves did not quite
suffice to cover her arms. She did not join her
companion, but strode briskly forward ; it was
the duty of the other to keep always at her
side.

The evening was lively, for there was pleasant weather for the first time after some blus-
tering days. But as the princess advanced all

conversation stopped only to begin again, when
she had passed, with a tumultuous current, like
a stream that had been dammed up and let loose
again. Princess Theresa Leaney participating
in the evening promenade ! Princess Theresa
Leaney on the Corso! And *how?* Radiant with
beauty, wealth, graciousness, with a friendly
look for all, she saluted the ladies she had been
in the habit of seeing from childhood up, the
merchants she had dealt with, the noblemen and
officers she had conversed with. In this the most
renowned of all Italian towns for the beauty of
its women, she did not, to be sure, carry off the
palm ; nevertheless, far and near she had been
surnamed " the beauty from Ancona," and the
town had for many years been ready to lower
its banner and join in the anthem of homage
whenever she wished.   And now she was willing.   There was a look of insinuating entreaty
in the eyes with which she smiled a greeting on
her " people," something apologetic in the bow
with which the smile was accompanied.   As
she returned she remarked the change in the
sentiments of her subjects, and ventured to
pause and converse with the members of one
of the oldest noble families of the town.   They
were sitting in front of a café in the middle of
the Corso. They received her with surprise,

yet courteously; she cared for the rest herself. The old gentleman, who was the head of the family, became more and more fascinated the longer she remained, and took pride and delight in presenting every one to her. She had a friendly greeting for all, was witty, joyous, and divided her attentions equally between the ladies and the gentlemen, until an atmosphere was created that finally became laden with merriment. The group kept constantly increasing in size, and when she moved away a large triumphal procession and loud-voiced conversation accompanied her. It might be said that the Corso was that evening the scene of a festival of universal reconciliation between the best society of the town and this its comely child, and it seemed as though both parties were alike happy therein.

The evening was advancing when she, and her followers with her, rose once more from champagne and ices; it was for the third time. She found no rest very long in any one place. Gayly but slowly the party moved on up the street. Three officers came walking along, somewhat covered with dust, and with rapid steps; they were evidently returning from a long expedition. The companion found her way, as by chance, to the side of the princess, and whispered something in her ear. The princess looked up, and at once recognized the form — there came Mansana!

Quite as a matter of course the companion then glided over to the other side, and Theresa moved farther along toward the place she had left; it was so near the officers that the nearest one could have stroked her dress with his sabre had he chosen to come one step closer. Now the nearest one was Mansana. The princess saw that he recognized her; the light fell full on the spot. She observed that he was surprised. But she also noticed that the short vigorous face seemed, as it were, to close itself, that the small deep eyes at once became veiled. He had the considerate tact not to appear to recognize her. She gave him a look for *that* and for his silence, besides — her large dark eyes sparkled, — a look that went to his heart and kindled there a fire that burst in flames over his cheeks. He walked on, no longer able to fix his thoughts on the conversation of his comrades. He was obliged, too, to take the express train early that night in order to follow his father's bones, the next day, to their grave of honor in his native place. No one deemed it singular that he went home early.

CHAPTER V

THE next day, as we have before seen, he
followed his father's bier with a desire, seem-
ingly, to leap far over and beyond it. That
one look bestowed on *him*, who had insulted
her, by Princess Theresa Leaney, in whom he,
in his proud defiance, had expected to find a
deadly enemy, that one look from out of all
her beauty and in the midst of her triumphal
progress on the Corso, had created a new image, and placed it on a pedestal within his soul.
It was the image of the princess herself, as
life's own victory-radiant goddess. Before this
pure, sublime beauty, all calumny sank away
as the feeble, vain efforts of a petty soul, and
his own conduct seemed like a presumptuous,
contemptible piece of brutality. Was it *she* he
had dared frighten and pursue?

And the development that had led him to
such profanation, that is to say, his own hard
life experience, he now tore asunder, link by
link, as he followed his father's bier, beginning with his father himself. For from his
father this dangerous inheritance of defiance
had been transmitted to his soul, where it had
taken root. It had inspired him with an ego-

tistic, savage will; he had most truly been his own model in every respect. Had his father been anything very different?

His noble and beautiful mother had so often wept as she sat alone with her children; her tears were an accusation against the man who had forsaken wife, child, and property to follow — what? — his defiance, his ambition, his revenge, which so often are the unruly comrades of patriotism, becoming at last its masters. He knew this to be so from his own experience and from that of hundreds of others who were now passed in review, one by one.

The music pealed forth, the cannons roared, the air was filled with cries of *Evviva* and flowers in honor of his father's memory.

" What hollowness in such a life," thought the son: " from conspiracy to prison, from prison to conspiracy again, while mother, wife, and child tread the path to poverty; while property is sold and nothing gained except the restless heart's rapid flight from suffering in revenge to revenge in suffering again. And this suffering was the inheritance of my childhood — and with it an empty life!"

And his father's old friends gathered about him to press his hand. They congratulated him on his father's honor, they even congratulated him on being the worthy heir.

" Aye, my life has been as hollow as his," he continued in his thoughts. " Swayed by a delight in revenge, as long as there was war, a restless craving for adventure of necessity followed, a vain ambition, a conceited sense of invincibility became the controlling element of life — brutal, selfish, hollow, all of it." And he vowed that henceforth his comrades should have something else to talk about than Giuseppe Mansana's last exploit, and that he himself would strive for a nobler pride than that caused by being sated with the consciousness that *he* never spoke of himself.

The nearer they drew to Mansana's birthplace, the more exultant became the throng and the more eager to see Giuseppe, the martyr's celebrated son. But to him, here on the play-grounds of his childhood, it seemed as if his grandmother once more sat on the curb-stone and was now casting stones at the procession : she was stoning that which had trampled under foot her life with all that she had gathered about her to make it happy.

Yet when his mother's grave, troubled eye rested on him, her gaze seemed almost an insult. *She* did not know what thoughts he had just been cherishing about all this, and about his own life as a continuation of his father's.

Why should she give him so anxious a look, when he had just bidden farewell to the temptations of a passion for honor? And he returned her gaze defiantly, for it did not strike home to him.

CHAPTER VI.

Two days later Mansana stood on the heights by the wall surrounding the ancient cathedral of Ancona. Neither on the noseless red marble lions that are the bearers of the porch pillars, nor on the glorious bay lying at his feet, did he bestow a look. His eye, indeed, glided over the decks of the ships and boats of lading below, as well as over the busy life in the arsenals and about the wharves; but his thoughts still lingered in the cathedral where he had just been himself, for there he had seen *her*. A solemn festival had called her thither. He had seen her kneel, and what was more, she had seen him! Aye, she had evidently been glad to see him, and had given him the same indescribable look as on that ever memorable evening. He could not gaze at her any longer without being obtrusive or attracting attention, and, besides, the incense-laden air and the dim, religious light had become unbearable to him. Here, though, it was fresh and free, and thoughts of beautiful objects could float about amid the beauty of the surrounding scene. Behind him he heard the people leaving the church; he saw them again in the windings of the road below, on foot and in carriages: he would not glance round, he was waiting until he could see *her* below him. Suddenly he heard steps approaching of one, of two persons; his heart throbbed, a mist gathered before his eyes; for the whole world he would not have turned. Some one paused at his side, also in front of the wall. He felt who it was and could not refrain from turning without appearing discourteous. She, too, was now gazing out over the ships, the bay, and the sea, but observed at once that he had changed his position. Her face was flushed, but she colored still more deeply as she smiled and said, —

"Pardon me for seizing this opportunity. I saw you, and I *must* express my thanks."

She ceased. She wanted to say more, he was sure of that. It did not come at once, it was quite an eternity before it came. But at last he heard the words : —

" There are times when nothing could be more magnanimous than silence. Thank you!"

She bowed forward, and he again ventured to look up. What grace ! What a smile was hers, as she glided away, followed by her companion ! What a walk, what a noble form ! And her long veil floated about in the wind, playing against her red velvet dress.

The road leading down from the heights is a winding one ; her carriage, which had halted at some distance, now drove up toward her and turned below the upper wall. But she had not reached it before she too heard footsteps behind her, almost running steps ; she stood still and looked round ; she knew who it was. She met his impetuosity with a smile, doubtless to set him at his ease.

" I did not at once fully comprehend," said he, as he bowed to her, while a deep flush overspread his bronzed face. " But it was by no means out of consideration that I was silent, it was from pride. I will not appropriate an honor I do not in the least deserve. And pardon me for my rudeness."

There was a tremor in his deep-toned voice ; he spoke with an effort ; Mansana was not a man of words. As he touched his hat, however, to make his parting salutation, his hand trembled, and this, as well as what had gone before, gave the princess an impression of great eloquence.

And thus it came to pass that Princess Theresa was attracted by so much frankness, and felt a desire to reward it; for what discoveries had not she also made about herself. And thus it happened, furthermore, that Princess Theresa did not step into her carriage, but walked past it between Captain Mansana and her companion. Thus also it chanced that she retraced her steps at his side, and that for more than an hour they walked back and forth at the foot of the upper wall, with the glorious view below them.

And when finally after she had taken her seat in the carriage and was being whirled round the curve leading into the lower road that ran parallel with the one she had just left, she once more sent him a bow and a smile in response to his renewed salutation, — he continued his march to and fro in the same spot for another hour. The sharp outlines of the bay, the verdure-clad slope of the mountains, the blue infinity of the sea, the sails dotted over the latter, and the columns of smoke in the horizon, — beautiful indeed is the bay of Ancona!

Through this unpremeditated encounter she

had gained about the same knowledge that he had gained; the history of her past had been very similar to that of his; she had told him so in acknowledging her vain defiance, her struggling ambition : with suppressed exultation, he had received this confession, word by word, from her lips.

Yonder image of beauty, far, far beyond *his* plane of existence, *now* hovered smiling about him, full of faults and yearnings like his own, but encircled by a halo of loveliness and glory into which he felt himself uplifted.

Oh, the Bay of Ancona! how bold its windings, how keenly blue-black the bosom of its waters in a breeze, how soft the transitions of color out upon the sea, terminating in a luminous haze!

CHAPTER VII.

WHAT was it that prevented him from presenting himself forthwith at her palace? A secret hope that she might once more appear to him. A vanity as long buried within the heart and nurtured in secret as Mansana's had been, is capable of the most astonishing surprises; it

can, in fact, be both shy and daring at the same
time.   He was really too shy to seek her, notwithstanding her invitation ; and yet he was
bold enough to believe that she would herself
come to the place where she had last met him.
He went every day to mass, but she did not
come ; and when he met her accidentally by
the sea, and on foot, he saw that she was either
embarrassed or displeased at his non-appear-
ance, he could not understand which.

Too late he discovered that in cherishing a
hope founded on his vanity, he had set aside
all common politeness.   He hastened to the
palace and sent in his card.

An old Italian palace which often has a
foundation wall built in the days of the great
empire, an interior dating back to the Middle
Ages or transition period, an exterior with fa-
çade and portico from the days of the renais-
sance, or a period directly following, and whose
ornamentations and furniture belong to quite as
many ages, while the statues, carvings, mova-
bles, may be traced back, the first to the plun-
derings of the Crusaders in the Greek islands
and in Constantinople, the rest to the Byzantine
period, and thence carried down to the present
day, — such an Italian palace, which can only
be found in seaport towns, is a fragment of the

history of civilization as well as that of a family; and it produces a strong impression on him who enters it, especially if he be one who was born among the people and is endowed with keen powers of observation. It also invests her who is established therein as the mistress of the triumphal hall of her ancestors, with a consciousness which imparts to friendliness something condescending, to politeness something aristocratic; but even this is not needed to remove her to a great distance from one who approaches her with an evil conscience. The surroundings in such an instance have a terribly subduing effect: even the familiar intercourse of a few preceding interviews cannot prevent the grand stairways, the lofty apartments, the history of a thousand years, from intimidating one who passes through the portal with a breach of courtesy on his conscience. If in addition to all this one's imagination has pictured somewhat closer relations with the mistress of the palace, that same imagination will frighten one away to a greater distance than needful.

Thus it came to pass that the first meeting proved a failure. Mansana was invited to call again, and did so with the embarassing sense that the previous interview had been awkward; consequently the second call turned out badly.

5

Afterward he met the princess with his wounded vanity on guard — and saw her smile.

All his proud defiance then returned. But what could he do? Here he dared not swear, not even speak; he was silent; he suffered, he went away, came again, and became aware that she was toying with his agony! Had she once felt herself vanquished, she now learned the relish of conquering her victor: she was treading familiar paths, and thus she bore herself with entrancing superiority.

Never did captured lion so tug at his chains as did Giuseppe Mansana at the delicate network of ceremonials and patronizing condescension that surrounded him. Nevertheless, it was impossible for him to remain away. In the frenzy of his nights and the soul-consuming mad chase, round and round in the same circle, by day, his strength was exhausted. Humility took possession of him.

He could not bear to hear her discussed by others; and he himself dared not mention her name lest he should betray his passion and become an object of derision. He could not brook seeing her in the society of others; and he himself dared not associate with her lest he should be compelled to undergo some humiliation. Not once, but a hundred times he felt a desire to slay both her and whoever for the moment she preferred to him, but was forced to control himself and go away. He was thoroughly convinced that this must lead to insanity or death, perhaps to both.

Yet so utterly powerless was he to struggle against his danger that at times he would lie flat on the ground in order to present to himself a picture of his own utter helplessness.

Why not end his career in some deed, some brilliant deed of revenge, worthy of his past? But, like thunder-clouds above a mountain, thoughts like these glided across his soul while it was in the fetters of Nature's law.

At last he was formally bidden to Princess Theresa's palace. One of the most celebrated musicians of Europe, returning that autumn from still farther south, passed through Ancona, and stopped there to pay his respects to the princess, whose acquaintance he had made in Vienna. She invited all the *élite* of Ancona to a superb festival, the first she had given in her palace. The arrangements were worthy of her wealth and station; universal joy prevailed, bearing along in the current the invalid master himself, who took a seat at the piano and began to play. The first note he struck had power to transform the entire assemblage into a group of friends, as often happens when beauty removes all restraints.

Theresa's eyes sought those of others, in order that she, too, might give and receive; and as her gaze wandered around it fell on Mansana, who in complete self-forgetfulness had pressed forward and was standing close beside the piano. The master was playing a composition entitled " Longing," in which out of the most profound anguish there was a reaching upward for consolation. He played like one who had known sorrow that bore him to the brink of despair. Never had the princess beheld a countenance like Mansana's at this moment. It was harder than usual, aye repulsively hard ; and yet tear after tear rolled in rapid succession down his cheeks. He looked as if he were bracing himself with an iron will, in order not to break down, and at the same time he gave the impression of trying to force back his tears. She had never seen anything so full of contradiction and so wretched. She gazed intently at him, and becoming overwhelmed at last by a strange dizziness that even caused her to believe that it was he who was in danger of falling, she rose to her feet. A loud burst of applause brought her to her senses, at the same moment so far withdrawing all eyes from her that she gained time to compose herself and wait until she could again safely dare to look up and endeavor to draw a long breath.

The composition was not quite ended, but she saw Mansana steal toward a door; doubtless the applause had startled him, too, and led him to the discovery that he was unable to control his emotions.

Her terror of a moment since still tingling through her veins, she abruptly sped through the listening multitude, to the astonishment of all, and passing out of the nearest door, hastened onward as though it depended on her to hinder a misfortune, — not without a feeling of guilt, not without a feeling of responsibility. As she had expected, he stood in the ante-room, where he had just thrown his cloak over his shoulders; his hat was already on his head. None of the servants were at hand, for they too had taken the liberty to listen to the music, and so she walked rapidly forward.

" Signore ! "

He turned, met her flashing eyes, and saw her excitement, as with both hands she stroked back the stray locks from cheeks and neck, a movement which with her always betokened decision but at the same time invested her form with its highest beauty.

" The train yesterday brought me the new Hungarian horses I told you about lately. To-morrow we must try them. Pray, will not you do me the kindness to drive for me ? Will you not ? "

His bronzed skin grew pale; she heard his rapid breathing. But he neither looked up nor spoke, he merely bowed in acquiescence. Then he laid his hand on the artistically wrought door handle, which yielded with a sonorous sound.

" At four o'clock," she added, hurriedly.

He bowed once more without raising his eyes, but in the open door he turned toward her again, hat in hand, proudly erect. This was his farewell. He saw her bestow on him a questioning look. *His* countenance might have called this forth. It certainly could not have concealed the flash of inspiration which illumined his gloomy mind, for now the knowledge had come to him how all this was to end.

CHAPTER VIII.

AT four o'clock the next day he was ushered by a servant through the ante-room and mirrored salon into the concert hall, and onward to one of the interior gothic rooms, where lay scattered the photographs of the last journey. It was announced to him that the princess would be ready immediately.

She made her appearance in a sort of Hungarian or Polish costume; the weather was rather chilly now in November, and especially to-day. She wore a close-fitting velvet dress, with a sable-edged sacque, which reached to the knees, on her head was a high, sable-trimmed cap, her hair floated loose.

As she gave him her hand, which was cased in a white glove, whose sable heading was bordered with lace, it was with the same firm, confiding trust to which eyes, face, aye, the voluptuous form itself, bore witness. *It could not be otherwise!* At all events, *his* interpretation was that she wanted to manifest a confidence she did not possess. This was confirmed by her soon lightly observing that perhaps it might be as well to postpone the drive: the horses had not yet recovered from the shock of their railroad travel. With cold derision he dismissed her fears. She studied his face: it betokened excitement and suffering, but was otherwise a closed book — as it was wonderfully capable of appearing. His manner was distant but more decided than it had been for a long time. Word was brought that the horses were waiting without ; at the same moment the companion entered. Mansana offered the princess his arm; she took it. On the steps she again looked up in his face and thought she perceived a light in it. Now she was alarmed. At the carriage door, availing herself of the opportunity arising from the necessity of having the horses held while they got into the vehicle, she again said, —

" Is it not really too soon to drive with them ? Had we not better put it off until another time ? "

Her voice quivered as she spoke, and laying her trembling hand on Mansana's arm, she looked up trustingly into his eyes. His countenance became transformed under this look, his eyes darkened.

" I thought you would scarcely be willing to venture on a drive with me — a second time ! "

Blushing crimson, the princess jumped into the carriage. Pale as a corpse, rigid as a pole,

the companion followed; but as though bound
for the dance Mansana sprang lightly on the
box. No servant accompanied them, the carriage was a light one-seated vehicle.

As soon as the horses were set free, the danger became manifest; the animals stood on their
hind legs, one of them pulled in one direction,
one in another. It certainly took more than a
minute to drive through the gate. " Good
Heavens! to think that you should wish this!"
whispered the companion, her eyes fixed in deadly terror on the two animals, who reared and
plunged and reared again, received each a blow
with the whip, darted back, tried to spring to
one side, received another blow, drew back,
gained another blow, and finally started forward. The mode of applying the lash was evidently not the most approved in the world.

When the street was reached the two foreign
horses began to tremble and stamp on the
ground; the new objects about them, the new
sounds, the new coloring, the brilliant southern light and warm glow over everything,
frightened them. But Mansana's skill and
strength of arms kept them in a gentle walk
until they had passed the Cavour monument;
then they began gradually to break loose. Mansana looked over his shoulder and met Princess

Theresa's eyes, and now it was he who was happy and she who suffered.

What could have led her to the unlucky notion of planning this drive? No sooner had she proposed it than she regretted having done so. She had felt sure, the moment she detected that gleam in his eye yesterday, that he would use this drive as a punishment, and that too with the same merciless resolution he had shown before. Why, then, was she sitting here? While noting accurately every movement made by him, by the horses, she asked herself this question over and over again, not with a view of obtaining an answer, but because her thoughts *must* be active.

Forward sped the horses in the most rapid trot that was possible; nor did their speed slacken. Mansana finally looked round. It was a movement of exultation; his eyes shot fire. But this was only the momentary introduction to what followed. Raising his whip, and giving it a dexterous swing, he let it fall whizzing on the backs of both animals at once. No sooner did they hear its sound in the air than with a leap forward they broke into a gallop.

Not a sound from the two who sat within.

Then he repeated the feat, thereby completely maddening the horses.

The road began to wind up a steeper and steeper hill. And just at this point Mansana raised the whip for the third time, swung it over his head like a lasso, and let it fall.

Now this action, during this furious speed, at such a place, was clear as a lightning flash in its significance : it was not punishment he sought, it was death, — death with her !

If there be any faculty of our soul which testifies of its divine origin it is this : the amount of time and number of events it can compass in the second of a second. From the moment when the whip inscribed that jubilant arc in the air until it fell, Princess Leaney had not only discovered but had actually experienced their united lives, interpreted by the new light, and had gained certainty in regard to this silent, proud love of Mansana's, that made him ready to meet death with exultation when it could be shared with her, — and in that same second of a second she had both formed her resolve and carried it into execution.

For simultaneously with the fall of the whip he heard behind him the one word, " Mansana ! " — not uttered in terror or condemnation : no, it was a wild shout of joy. He whirled round ; there, in the midst of this tempestuous drive, she stood erect, with beaming

countenance and outstretched arms. More rapidly than it can be told, he had turned toward
the horses, thrown aside the whip, wound the
reins three times around his arms, and, strain-
ing every nerve, braced himself against the
dash-board of the carriage. He would live with
her.

Now, indeed, a desperate struggle ensued.
He had resolved to turn the course of death's
bridal procession into that of life.

In a whirling cloud of dust, on the very brink
of the precipice, they dashed stormily onward ;
the foaming horses could be forced to hold their
heads higher, so that their manes fluttered behind them, like sable pinions, — that was all.
At last Mansana grasped the right rein with
both hands, in order to guide the mad race into
the middle of the road, — taking his chance
about encountering whatever obstacle might be
in the way ; for at all events they should pass
proudly through the portal of death. He succeeded in getting the horses into the middle of
the road, but their speed was not checked, —
and lo ! far beyond he thought he descried a
mass of objects approaching ; the whole road
was blocked up by it. A nearer view proved it
to be one of those interminable herds of cattle
which in the autumn are driven to the seashore.

Then he started to his feet, flinging the reins over the dash-board. A loud shriek behind him ! He leaped forward ; still another piercing shriek ; but he was already on the back of the right horse, grasping the other by the bit. The one on which he was sitting sprang into the air while still running, whereby it was thrown down by the other horse. It was nevertheless carried along for some distance by the outer thill until this broke beneath the burden, and was then still dragged onward until the neck-yoke also gave way. Mansana's grasp of the bit saved him, and together with the weight of the disabled horse, brought the race to an end. But the fallen horse felt the carriage upon it and kicked out wildly ; the one standing reared ; the carriage pole snapped, one piece struck Mansana on the side, yet he did not relax his hold, and was now in front of, or rather under, the standing horse, with a cruel grip in its nostrils, until it became as meek as a captured, trembling lamb. He was up himself in a moment ; the prostrate horse, which had made several dangerous attempts to rise, was helped.

And now, thickly covered with dust, tattered and torn, bleeding, hatless, Mansana for the first time ventured to look up and about him.

Theresa was standing at the open carriage door. She must have been about to jump out and have been cast back by one of the terrible shocks they had experienced, and have started to her feet again, — or something to that effect; she herself knew not how it had happened. But what she now did fully comprehend was that *he* stood there safe, holding the shivering horses by the bits.

Out of the carriage and toward him she sprang; and he turned to receive her with wide open arms; she flung herself into them! Bosom was strained to bosom, lip sought lip, and thus these lofty forms stood wrapped each in the other's embrace. And this seemed as though it would never end. The arms did not relax, not even to renew their clasp, neither were lips nor eyes withdrawn; hers only sank deeper into his.

The first word that was spoken was a whispered " Theresa ! " Then their lips were again sealed.

Never did woman with greater rejoicing accept the place of ruler than she that of subject when this embrace at last came to an end. Never did fugitive, with such prodigiously sparkling, joyous eyes, beg pardon for having struggled for freedom. Never before did

princess plunge with such zeal into her duties
as a slave, as did she, when she discovered his
wound, his torn and dust-covered condition.
With her delicate white hands and her rich
handkerchief and pins, she began to cleanse,
bind up, and fasten together, and with her eyes
she healed and made whole, — perhaps not the
wounds, and yet it really was the wounds, for
he felt them no more.

For each little service, there was an added
caress, fresh silent or spoken joy. Finally they
so entirely forgot carriage, horses, and companion, that they betook themselves on their way
toward town, as though there remained to them
nothing more than to press onward with their
new-found happiness. A cry of alarm from the
companion and the slowly approaching herd
awakened them.

CHAPTER IX.

THEIR blissful intoxication neither ended
that day nor the days that immediately followed. The higher circles of Ancona were
drawn into it, since the betrothal was celebrated

with fêtes and excursions. There was indeed
something startlingly romantic in the whole affair. Mansana's fame, the wealth, rank, and
beauty of the princess; *she* the hitherto invin-
cible, *he* the ever victorious; and then even the
circumstances attending the betrothal, that in
the mouths of the people had acquired the most
incredible embellishments, — all this combined
to heighten one degree Princess Theresa's fe-
licity, surrounding it with a truly magic halo.

When these two were seen together, a fine
contrast was presented by them. They were
both tall, they had the same elastic step and
proud carriage; but her face was long, his
short; her eyes were large and wide-open, his
small and deep. One could not but admire her
delicate, long nose, pouting lips, noble chin,
beautifully arched cheeks, encircled by black
hair; but his low brow, small, firmly compressed mouth, defiant chin, shortly-cropped
hair, did not invest him with beauty. Quite
as great was the difference between her out-
wardly-manifested joy, her brilliant discourse,
and his taciturn manner.

But neither she nor their friends would have
had him otherwise, not even at such a time as
this; for he was true to his nature. Why,
even matters on which he was ready to stake

his life became transformed into every-day commonplaces when he allowed himself to talk about them ; but as a rule he did not talk.

And so neither the princess nor the social circle in which she and Mansana moved, perceived that now, aye, at this very time, he was undergoing a great change.

There is a certain boundless submission, a jealous zeal in rendering service, which converts the recipient into a slave or a mere tool. Not a moment's liberty, not a particle of freedom of will is allowed to remain. The slightest expression of anything of the kind calls forth twenty new plans for the attainment of what is desired and a tumult of passionate actions.

There is a way of giving confidence which insinuates itself into those precincts of our soul where mortal has never penetrated before — divines thoughts, brings to light reflections, and is exceedingly embarrassing to one who has been in the habit of living shut up within himself.

Such and more was the case in regard to Mansana. Within a few days he was satiated ; the ineffable exhaustion resulting from excitement, that of despair as well as that of joy, made him doubly irritable. There were moments when he abhorred the sight both of her and of society.

6

He was shocked himself at this as at the blackest ingratitude, and in the honesty of his soul he finally confessed it to her. He gave her some idea of what he had suffered, and how near destruction he had been, showing her that this excess of mad public festivity was just the opposite of what he needed. He could bear no more.

She was deeply moved by this revelation. In the midst of a cloud of the wildest self-accusations, she decided on rest for him, departure for herself. *She* would go to Rome and Hungary to make arrangements for the wedding; *he* should go to a mountain fortress farther south, where he could exchange with an officer who wanted to be in Ancona. She was so strong she speedily carried this plan into execution. Within two days both he and she had left the place. The parting on her side was very affecting; on his, truly heartfelt: her love and ardor touched him.

But no sooner was he alone, first on the journey and afterward in the garrison, than he sank into a state of complete apathy. He had scarcely any other recollection of her than a confused tumult of impressions. He could not even prevail on himself to open the letters that came from her; he shrank from her vehemence.

The fact was she telegraphed and wrote at least once each day, and when his obligations to reply pressed too heavily upon him, he fled from his own room, where all lay unfulfilled and waiting. When not on duty, therefore, he wandered about in the woods and hills beyond the town, for the country was unusually wild and beautiful in this vicinity.

On these excursions he could dissolve all he had been through into a species of illusion. The title of principessa-eccellenza has not the same charm in Italy as elsewhere; there are too many who bear it, some of them occupying questionable positions. Nor had the fortune inherited by Theresa from her father anything alluring about it, for it had been gained by her mother through treachery to the fatherland in its period of degradation. Neither did Theresa's beauty continue to hold sway, for it was beginning to grow too ripe. Their romantic meeting no longer sufficed to wipe out the long humiliation she had at first permitted him to endure, and her final abandonment left behind a sense of *ennui*. In stronger moments, however, Mansana's dream-images strove to attain different forms, but then his pride revolted and assured him that in a union with Princess Leaney he must always be the inferior, perchance in the end the toy of her caprices. Had he not already been so ?

After his morning walk he usually rested on a bench beneath an old olive-tree, just beyond the town. From there he walked down to his breakfast. One morning he saw two people, an elderly gentleman and a young lady, take their seats on the bench as he left it. The same thing occurred the next morning and at the same hour. The day following this he kept his seat rather longer than usual, not without design, and thus had an opportunity to look at the young lady and talk with the old gentleman. The facility with which Italians enter into a conversation and an acquaintance soon made him possessor of the facts that the gentleman was a pensioner from the past administration ; that the young lady was his daughter, was about fifteen years of age, and was just out of a convent. She kept very close to her father and spoke but little, yet Mansana thought she had the sweetest voice he had ever heard.

Afterward they met every day and not by chance. He always waited on the heights until he saw them coming up from the town, and then he approached the bench. They were both very friendly and quiet. The old gentleman fell into the habit of talking a little every day, in a timid way, about politics; when he was through Mansana would exchange a few words with the daughter. She was the living image of her father. He had been corpulent; his face still preserved a certain wrinkled plumpness. She would become just like him, for her little dumpy figure gave promise of this; it possessed, however, that budding fullness to which a morning dress is so becoming, and Mansana never saw her in anything else. The father's eyes were feeble and watery; hers were half closed, her head, too, she kept slightly bowed. The little individual's face and figure had great powers of attraction in this quiet intercourse. Her hair was carefully done up, day after day, in the latest style; this betrayed a desire on the part of the child of the cloister to be one with this wicked world. Those small plump hands that were so well poised on the firmly-knit wrists, were always busied with some dainty bit of needle-work which the head was bowed over and the half-closed eyes followed. She raised the drooping lids when Mansana addressed her, but usually bestowed only a side glance on him, although she did not wholly look away. The yet undeveloped soul of a child peeped forth from her eyes half shyly,

half joyously, but with thorough curiosity, on
the new world she had entered, and on this new
person she had found in it. The more one
gazes into such half-closed eyes, the more they
fascinate, inasmuch as they never wholly reveal
their hidden depths. So far as hers were concerned, there was often something roguish lurk-
ing in their corners, and what they actually
thought of *him* — aye, that Mansana would
have given much to know. And simply in
order to gain favor in her eyes he told her
more about himself than he had ever in his life
told to any one person. It diverted him to
watch her two dimples coming and going while
he talked, and the continual play about the
small mouth, which was as red and as sweet
as an untouched berry.

But it diverted him still more when, with a
voice whose innocent tones rang in his mind
like the warbling of birds on a parched summer
morning, she began bashfully but inquisitively
to question him about his approaching marriage. Her ideas concerning betrothals and
wedding-trips, if not directly expressed, at least
peeping out all over her questions, were so
enchanting that they restored the old charm to
the subject itself.

To *her* it was due that ten or twelve days

after his arrival in this place Theresa actually received a letter from him, and immediately afterward several others.

He was no master of the pen ; his letters, therefore, were as brief as his conversations ; that they became ardent was due again to the little one. Every morning after breakfast he wrote ; the fact was, he took so lively a pleasure in those innocent morning conversations, surveying the fresh girlish form, the deft fingers that were engaged in the needle-work, the harmony of mouth, eyes, and dimples, enjoying the tones of her voice, that all his old yearnings were revived.

Quite a contrast to the little one did Theresa present in all her superb grandeur of body and mind, when he sat at his desk holding converse with her. Even now he could not smile at her vehemence, yet how magnanimous was her acceptance of his silence : —

" It did not worry me in the least. *Of course you should not have written!* You needed rest even from me ; you ought to have been free from my letters, too, at all events from their impetuosity. But forgive me! This is *your* fault alone, as *I* alone am to blame for what you now suffer. I can never forgive myself, but will endeavor to make amends to you through all the rest of my life! "

Not one in a thousand would have thought and written thus; he was forced to admit this to himself — and at the same time that she always exhausted him. In order to become more composed and calm, he wrote her about Amanda Brandini, — that was the young girl's name.

He repeated a conversation the little one had had with him about weddings and marriages. It seemed to him very attractive, and he thought he had expressed it so well that he could not help reading the letter over a second time.

The sprightly morning meetings, over which he rejoiced the whole day long, were never followed by an invitation to visit father and daughter in their own home. This honorable reserve pleased Mansana and the interviews awakened ever greater and greater longings for Theresa. How unspeakably was not the princess surprised when she received a telegram announcing that he would meet her in Ancona in three days, — he yearned for her.

The day the telegram was sent he happened to be lounging about a square, on which was a café, and feeling thirsty he entered it. He sat looking out on the square, while waiting to be served, — he had never been there before. Suddenly he discovered Amanda Brandini on a balcony opposite. So that was where she lived.

But at her side and leaning over the railing, as she was doing, and so near her that he could breathe her breath, stood a gay young lieutenant. He had been presented that same forenoon to Mansana, who had heard that he was from a neighboring garrison, and that he was usually called " the Amorin."

But now " the Amorin's " eyes hung on hers ; they were both smiling, while their lips moved, and as what they were saying could not be heard it looked to Mansana as though they were whispering confidentially together. They never seemed to get through.

Giuseppe Mansana felt the blood rush to his heart, and he experienced a burning pain. He rose and strode away, then remembered that he had not paid for what he had left behind untouched, turned and settled his account. When he got outside and again looked up, he was surprised to see the two in the balcony engaged in wrestling. " The Amorin " was urging something, she was defending herself, as red as blood. The struggle set off her figure, her eagerness, her face. " The Amorin's " insolent assurance called forth a tumultuous opposition. Who had admitted such a house-breaker? Where was her father?

CHAPTER X.

THE next morning Mansana sat earlier than was his wont on the bench ; but the other two also came earlier. They, too, must find satisfaction in the interviews and desire to prolong them, now that but two yet remained. From the inevitable political introduction with the father, he suddenly turned toward Amanda with, —

" Who was that you were wrestling with on the balcony yesterday ? "

Her face became suffused with the loveliest blushes, while her eyelids drooped even more than usual ; still she tried to look at him.

A young girl blushes, indeed, at everything, but this Mansana did not know. He grew quite as pale as she was rosy. This alarmed her ; he saw it, and misinterpreted this also.

The father, who had been listening with open mouth, broke out, —

" Ah, now I understand ! Luigi, my sister's son, Luigi Borghi ! Yes, he is in town on a visit of a few days ; will remain for the town festival. Ha, ha, he is a madcap ! "

But Giuseppe Mansana went straight from this interview to his friend Major Sardi, the man for whose sake he had chosen this especial garrison, and asked him about Luigi's character. It was bad.

Thence he went to the young man himself, who lived at a hotel and had just risen. Luigi Borghi greeted his superior officer respectfully and with many apologies. They both took seats.

" I leave here to-morrow to be married," began Mansana. " I mention this in order that what I am about to say may be understood — as it is meant. I have, during my brief sojourn here, taken a great liking to an innocent young girl. Her name is Brandini."

" Ah, Amanda ! "

" She is your cousin ? "

" Yes, she is."

" Do you stand in any other relation to her ? Do you intend to marry her ? "

" No — but " —

" I have no other motive in questioning you about this than that of a gentleman. You need not reply, if you object."

" Certainly not ! I repeat it with pleasure : I do not intend to marry Amanda ; she is very poor."

" Very well. Why, then, do you go as you do to the house ? Why do you call forth sentiments in her to which you have no thought of responding, and which may so easily be misinterpreted?"

"Your last remark seems to me to imply an accusation."

"To be sure. You are known to be a reckless libertine."

"Signore!" and the young lieutenant rose to his feet.

At once the tall captain did the same.

"I, Giuseppe Mansana, say this, and am at your service."

But little Luigi Borghi had no fancy to be slain at such an early and interesting age by the first fencer in the army. And so he was silent, and his eyes sought the ground.

"Either you will promise me never to enter her house again, never to seek her society, or you will have to answer for your conduct to me. I have resolved to settle this before I leave. Why do you hesitate?"

"Because, as an officer, I cannot be known to have been compelled"—

"To do a good deed? You may thank your God if you can be! Perhaps I have presented the subject in the wrong way. I should undoubtedly have said to you: 'Do what I ask of you, and you shall be my friend, and may count on me in whatever straits you may come ! ' "

" I would gladly have for my friend so great an officer, and would be proud to be able to count on Giuseppe Mansana's generous aid."

" Very well. Then you promise what I ask ? "

" I promise ! "

" Thank you ! Your hand ! "

" With all my heart ! "

" Farewell ! "

" Farewell ! "

Two hours later Mansana went down to the toledo of the little town. There, outside of a shop, stood Amanda and Luigi, engaged in a conversation which seemed to be highly entertaining to both, for they were laughing heartily. The father was inside of the shop, paying for some purchases. None of them saw Mansana until he was in their midst. His pale, sallow face sufficed to send Amanda flying in terror to her father ; but the still more appalled lieutenant remained where he was and said, retreating a step, —

" I assure you, signore, I was requested to come here ! And we — we were not laughing at you."

At that moment a shriek from Amanda rang

out of the shop. It was caused by Giuseppe Mansana's appearance, as he, without a word, without a gesture, made a stride forward, just one, toward her little cousin. There was a leopard's seven-ells leap in this stride ; the next moment Luigi might be a dead man.

But every one in the shop and on the street turned to the young girl who had uttered the shriek, and who stood nestled up to her father. From her the eyes of the by-standers wandered in all directions. There was nothing to be seen. Two officers stood quietly outside in the street conversing together. What was the matter ? Those who were outside came into the shop, and all gathered about Amanda. What was it ? But she, exposed, for the first time in her life, to the gaze and questions of the multitude, stood aghast, and her father, who had failed to obtain an answer, became bewildered. Then Mansana parted asunder the group about her, and with a silent air of command offered her his arm; she hastened to accept it and walked away with him ; her father followed.

When they were out of ear-shot, Mansana said, —

"It is my duty to tell you that your kinsman, Lieutenant Borghi, is a profligate wretch, who deserves and shall receive chastisement."

How alarmed Amanda was again : first to hear that Luigi was a profligate wretch, although she did not exactly know what that meant, and next that Luigi was to receive chastisement, although she knew not why. She gazed this time with wide-open eyes into Mansana's face ; but looked none the wiser. Her lips, too, parted. A great curiosity began to break through her fear ; Mansana detected it, — and angry as he had just been he now could not but smile at such intensely stupid innocence, and its ludicrous and bewitching expression. And thus suddenly thrown into a good-humor again, he even observed at last what a comical appearance the father presented. The old gentleman was like a school-boy who has been listening to ghost stories in the dark. In order to show Mansana how thoroughly he understood all that was horrible, he manifested a profound gratitude and begged him to accompany them home.

This Mansana did ; and Amanda, who hoped she might learn something more, clung to him in the most deferential and insinuating manner. He began by conjecturing her purpose, and it amused him ; but ended by forgetting this and feeling jubilant delight over the melodious murmur of her voice, over each roguish word, and at the thought that her sweet lips, about which the dimples came and went, her half-closed eyes, in their enigmatical play, and her harmonious nature, for one moment were wholly conse- crated to him, and that this fresh, youthful form, in all the fullness of its beauty, lived and breathed in his proximity.

The next morning their last interview was to take place; but no, it was not permitted to be the last; he must come to them the next after- noon, for he was not to leave until evening. He went from them in an ecstasy of delight.

The soothing influence she exercised over him, manifested itself also by impelling him to present himself that same afternoon in the un- fortunate Luigi's room and asking his pardon. *He* was not to blame for meeting his cousin in the street and being accosted by her.

" And if you were laughing at me " —

" But we were not, indeed ! " protested the frightened " Amorin."

" You surely had a right. My zeal was rather absurd. I am aware of it now. Here is my hand ! "

This was hastily seized, a few disconnected words were spoken, and Mansana left — in un- disputed supremacy, as he had come.

The little lieutenant, who had been feeling

like one who had death for his companion, was seized with a dizzy joy. He sprang up in the air and burst into the loudest peals of laughter. Mansana heard this laughter, and paused on the stairs. Luigi shuddered at his imprudence, and when there came once more a knock at the door he was too terrified to say, " Come in ! " But the door was opened, nevertheless.

" Was that you who were laughing ? " inquired Mansana.

" No, on my honor ! " replied the " Amorin," gesticulating with both hands. Mansana stood for a while contemplating him.

But when he was gone again, the exultation returned. Luigi could not help it. And as he dared neither scream nor dance, he *must* communicate it to some one. This he did at the officers' café among his former classmates. It created great merriment. Over the wine-cup witticisms fell like hail upon the unlucky captain, who on the eve of his wedding with a princess created a scandal by falling in love with a little boarding-school miss.

Major Sardi, Mansana's friend, was witness to this.

The next morning Mansana had his last interview on the heights. It began much earlier than usual, and ended much later, and not until

the door of father and daughter's house was
reached. In the afternoon he was to call according to promise to take leave. Half ro-
guishly, half languishingly, exactly as she felt
about it, Amanda discussed the wedding, for
to a well brought-up Italian girl marriage is
the portal that leads to all earthly bliss, that is
to the state in which uncertainty, restraint, and
annoyances cease, and in which perpetual peace,
new dresses, carriage drives, and evenings at
the opera begin! Her sweet babble was but
the song of his own longings ; her dainty little
person invested this song with increased fullness,
so that the realization of his approaching happiness impelled him to tell the young girl of the
part she had had in it. Little Amanda shed tears
at this, — a young girl's tears are so ready to
flow when anything kind is said about her. And
then she could not help telling him how much
confidence she felt in him. She mentioned this
because she had always been a trifle uneasy in
his presence ; but she did not say so. Since,
therefore, it was not as true as she would herself have wished, she added a smile. This was
to strengthen her words. But where the smile
shone the atmosphere was still full of tears,
and it formed there (I mean within Mansana's
own breast) an inconceivably beautiful rain-

bow. He took her round little hand in both
of his : that was his farewell. He said something, moreover, but knew not what himself ;
she grew rosy red. He saw her brow, arms,
and head above him on the stairs, and again
from the balcony. He heard floating out over
the square a melodious " Farewell ! " and still
another — and then he turned into a side
street.

He had not noticed the approach of Sardi,
had not seen that the latter was making directly for him, and he was roused in bewilder-
ment by a slap on the shouder.

" Is it really true ? " laughed Sardi. " Are
you in love with the little one up yonder ? —
you actually look so ! "

Mansana's face became copper-colored, his
eyes had a fixed stare, his breath came and
went hastily.

" What is that you say ? " asked he. " How
do you know " — He paused. He certainly
would not himself tell what he first wanted to
hear, whether any one could have — whether
Luigi had — " What is that you say ? " he repeated.

" Upon my soul ! You are not getting embarrassed ; are you ? "

" What is that you say ? " reiterated Mansana, redder than before, knitting his brow, and laying one hand, not very gently, on the major's shoulder.

This offended Sardi. Mansana's violence, indeed, came upon him so unexpectedly that he had no time for reflection ; but in self-defense, and in order to annoy the friend who had given way to so unjust an outburst of wrath, he repeated to Mansana what people already said, and how he had been made sport of at the officers' café.

Mansana's wrath knew no bounds. He swore that if Sardi did not forthwith state who had dared such a thing, he himself must give satisfaction for it. The two friends were actually on the verge of a challenge. But Sardi finally so far regained his self-possession that he was able to represent to the other what an unpleasant noise it would create if Mansana should fight with him or any one else about his correct relations with Amanda Brandini, and that, too, on the eve of his departure for his wedding with Princess Leaney. The best answer would certainly be to leave and celebrate his nuptials. Hereupon a fresh ebullition of wrath from Mansana. He was able to attend to his own affairs and defend his own honor. Out with the names ! Sardi could find no reason for concealing these, and gave them one by one, adding that if it would gratify him to kill all these young lads, he might if he chose! Mansana wanted to go forthwith to the officers' café, as though they were all still there. Sardi succeeded in convincing him of the folly of this; then he insisted upon at least seeking Borghi without delay. Now Sardi expressed a willingness to present a challenge to Borghi; " but," said he, " on what grounds should he be challenged."

" For what he has said! " shrieked the other.

" Why, what has he said? That you are in love with Amanda Brandini? And are you not ? "

Had Mansana set forth without meeting Sardi, he would have been married a few days later to Princess Leaney. Now, on the contrary, this was what took place : —

Mansana: " Do you presume to say that I love Amanda ? "

Sardi : " I merely ask. But if you do *not* love her, how the deuce does it concern you if the whelp does say so, or if he loves her himself — or leads her astray ? "

" You are a brutal scoundrel to speak so ! "

" Pray, what are *you* who attack a young relative merely because he jokes with her " —

" Jokes with her ! "

Mansana clinched his fists and pressed his lips together.

" Who will look after them when you are gone ? " Sardi hastened to remark.

" I am not going away ! " shrieked Mansana.

" Not going away ! Have you lost your senses ? "

" I am not going away ! " repeated Mansana, with hands and arms uplifted, as though he were taking a solemn oath.

Sardi was alarmed.

" Then you do love her, after all," he whispered.

Mansana gave way completely ! Deep groans were heard ; his powerful frame was shaken by them. Sardi feared a stroke of apoplexy. Finally Mansana seemed, as it were, to rise superior to himself, his countenance shone, and slowly, perfectly self-possessed, he said, —

" I love her ! " and then turning to Sardi : " I shall not leave ! "

And from this moment he was like a tempest : he turned, looked above and beyond him, and stormily sped onward.

" Where are you going ? " asked Sardi, hastening after him.

" To Borghi."

" But I thought I was to go to him ! "

" Then go ! "

" But where are *you* going ? "

" To Borghi ! " And pausing, he added, in an ecstasy, —

" I love her. Any one who wants to take her from me *shall die!* "

He was about to proceed on his way.

" But does *she* love you ? " shrieked Sardi, forgetting that they stood in the street.

Mansana stretched forth his sinewy hands and said in a hollow voice, —

" *She shall love me.* "

Sardi was frightened.

" Giuseppe, you are mad ! " said he. " The high pitch to which you have been worked up was more than you could bear. Now it has only assumed new force and centred in a new object. You are not yourself ! — Giuseppe — do not run away from me ! Can you not see that the people on the street are noticing you ? "

Then Mansana stood still.

" Do you know why I became ill, Cornelio ? Because I paid attention to the people on the street? I was *forced* to keep silent, to hear, to be trampled on ! That was what made me ill." He advanced a step nearer to Sardi.

" Now I will shriek it aloud to the whole world : I love her ! "

He actually did shriek aloud, then turned and walked on with a proud bearing. Sardi fol lowed and took him by the arm. He guided him into a still narrower street, but Mansana seemed wholly unconscious of it. He merely walked on, talking in a loud voice, and gesticulating.

" What would it be for me to become Princess Leaney's husband," said he, " and to be the manager of her ladyship's property and the servant of her ladyship's caprices ? "

And here he gave loose reins to his deeply wounded self-love.

" Now for the first time I admit to myself the whole truth : it would have been an unworthy life for Giuseppe Mansana."

Sardi thought that if the reticent and at least outwardly modest Giuseppe Mansana could suddenly begin thus to shout and boast, any other inconceivable thing might occur ; and with a perseverance and ingenuity that did him honor he endeavored to persuade his friend to take a short trip, if only for a couple of days, in order to gain light on the emotions and circumstances that were submerging him. But he might as well have talked at a hurricane.

CHAPTER XI.

THAT same evening Amanda, in the greatest secrecy, received a letter, which made her exceedingly curious. She struck a light and read it. It was from Luigi! — the first she had ever received from him. It read thus : —

AMANDA, — A madman is in pursuit of me and wants to kill me. An hour ago I was obliged to give him a solemn promise — indeed, I have signed my name to it — to relinquish all claims on you forever, and not even to speak to you! This was cowardice, I well know. I despise myself, as you must despise me.

But the way this came about was that not until I had given my word did I know that I loved you. Perhaps I did not do so before. But now I love you beyond all bounds, and never in the world has there been a more unhappy mortal than I am.

I cannot conceive of the possibility of its being all over! It cannot be so forever. It depends, though, altogether on yourself, Amanda, if you do not despise me too greatly. For if you love me the madman will accomplish nothing, and so some day things must change again.

I am like a man in prison. I cannot stir.
But this I know, that if you do not help me out
again, I shall die.

Amanda! A word, a sign! It is too dangerous to write. I know not how I shall manage to get this to you. Do not *you* try to send
a letter to me. He may be on the scent. But
to-morrow at the festival! Be there, near the
band, stay there until I have found you. Then
speak only with your eyes! If they are friendly,
I shall know all. Ah, Amanda, the rest will come
of itself when once you are mine! Amanda,

Your devoted and unhappy cousin,

LUIGI.

The moment Amanda had read this letter
she knew that she loved Luigi. Never before
had she looked into this matter. But now she
loved him beyond measure, of this she was
sure.

There must be some misunderstanding about
what Mansana had said concerning him, and
the promise Luigi had made of course did not
amount to anything. Girls do not accept such
things very literally when they seem improb-
able to them. Moreover, Mansana had now
gone away.

And so, the next day, the festival day, a

lovely autumn day, she was astir betimes in the
morning ; the band had passed at sunrise and
the cannons had sent forth their thundering
peals. The church, decorated within and without, was crowded, and little Amanda might be
seen at her father's side, among the worshipers,
dressed in her choicest finery. She prayed for
Luigi. When she had finished she practiced
smiling. She was resolved to offer Luigi consolation through the most friendly look she
could command. When the procession was
over and noon had passed, she hastened to the
appointed spot ; the band was already playing
on the market-place. She so urged her old
father on that they were among the first grown
people who arrived, but for that reason among
those who were most wedged in before an hour
had elapsed. She looked at her father's per-
spiring face and thought of her own and what
a horrid appearance it would present to Luigi.
She must get out of the crowd, let it cost what it
might ; and yet the price should not be a rose
or a knot of ribbon, or even the least exertion,
for that would cause her to grow redder than
she now was. She therefore made but little
progress.

Yet, alas ! she grew hotter and hotter. She
heard the big drum and a couple of bass horns,

through the thunder of thousands of voices **and** laughter in which she was submerged; she **saw** the tower on the municipal building, and **the** clapper which extended below the bell, **and** which was the last object she beheld above the human billows that closed about her. Her father's pitiable face told her how red and odious she must appear — and the little one began to weep.

But Luigi, too, had been among the first to reach the band; and as neither the town nor the square in front of the municipal building were large, the two who were seeking each other amid the thronging multitude could not well avoid at last standing face to face. He saw her, rosy with blushes, smiling through her tears. He took her blushes for those of joy, her tears for those of sympathy, and her smile for what it was intended. The father, in his anxiety and distress, hailed Luigi as an angel of deliverance and cried, —

"Help us, Luigi."

And Luigi promptly set to work to do as he was bid. The task was no easy one; indeed both Amanda and her father were several times in actual danger, and Luigi felt himself a hero. With elbows and back he defended them, and never once removing his eyes from Amanda, he drank deeply from her long, timid gaze. He did not speak; he did not break his oath! This, too, gave him a proud consciousness; there must be an air of nobility about him, and he felt from the reflection in Amanda's eyes that he really did appear noble.

But no earthly happiness is of long duration. Giuseppe Mansana had about a quarter of an hour previous to this descried Luigi in the crowd, and with the instinct that jealousy possesses, had watched him from afar, an easy matter for one of Mansana's height. Luigi, in his restless search, had constantly worked his way forward, and had thus no idea of the danger close at hand; and now he was so engrossed with his task of deliverance, or, in other words, in reflecting his noble image in Amanda's eyes, that he perceived nothing until Mansana's hyena face was directly opposite his, and he felt his scorching breath on his cheeks.

Amanda gave one of her well-known screams, her father became frightfully stupid, and Luigi disappeared.

At the same moment, Amanda had drawn one arm through Mansana's and placed the warm, gloved hand of the other on his; two bewitching, half-closed eyes, brimming over with roguishness, fear, and entreaty, looked up into his face. They were just out of the throng, it was possible to understand what was said, and Mansana heard from a voice, which might ring the angels into heaven, —

" Papa and I have been in great danger. It was so nice that we got help ! " and he felt the pressure of her hand.

Now Mansana had seen those same eyes dwelling on Luigi's face, and there rushed through his mind a thought which later in life he took up again a thousand times but now lost the moment it came, and this thought was, " I am certainly entangled in a stupid, meaningless affair."

The little prattler by his side continued, —

" Poor Luigi met us just at our extremity. Papa begged him to help us, and he did so without speaking a word. We did not even get to thank him." And directly after : " It is really delightful that you have not left yet. Now you must go home with us that we may have a good talk ! We had such a nice one the last time."

And her full, young bosom fluttered beneath its silken covering, her round wrist quivered above her glove, the tips of her little feet moved restlessly below her dress ; her rosy lips bubbled over with chatter and laughter, and those two eyes of hers beamed in half-concealed familiarity, — and Mansana was borne along with them.

He did not mention Luigi's name; it remained like a dagger-point in his heart; it entered the deeper the more charming she became. This struggle between pain and love made him absolutely silent. But all the busier were her sweet lips, while she gave him a seat and brought forward fruits, which she herself peeled and handed to him. She went into a little ecstasy of delight that their meetings on the heights were not yet interrupted; indeed, she proposed a little excursion farther up the slope, which they must make the next morning; she would bring breakfast along. Still he had only succeeded in uttering a few monosyllables. He could not break in upon this innocent idyl with his passion; and yet the struggle within was so terrible that he could bear it no longer, and was compelled to leave.

No sooner was he down the steps and the last greeting had been sent from the balcony, than the little charmer, who had been so unwearied in her flattering attentions, closed tightly the balcony door and flung herself sobbing on her knees before her father. He was not in the least surprised. He had the same fear as she;

Mansana's last look as he left, as well as his whole presence, had filled the room with such a fateful atmosphere, that if in the next moment they had all exploded it would not in the least have surprised him.   And when, through her tears, she whispered, " Father, we must leave here ! " he merely replied, " Yes, my child, of course we must ! "

It was essential to depart secretly, and therefore, if possible, that very night.

CHAPTER XII.

GIUSEPPE MANSANA had been at Borghi's room and had not found him ; at the officers' café and not found him ; later, about amongst the festal throng, but had met him nowhere. On the other hand, he had encountered many officers, and civilians, too, in company with them, who seemed to him to relapse into silence when they saw him, and to talk in low tones together as he passed them.

Whatever manner of game it might be that he was engaged in, lose he must not.   His honor forbade it.

Exhausted in body and soul, he sat late in the evening on the watch in front of the café, facing the Brandini apartment. There was a light in Amanda's window. She was packing up the few articles she and her father were to take with them, for in order to give their departure the appearance of a short trip they were to leave most of their things behind.

But Mansana thought: this light is perhaps a signal. And sure enough, when Amanda was weary from excitement and work, she went out on the balcony to take a few breaths of fresh air; she could be seen so plainly by the light behind her; she looked down along the street. Was she expecting any one from that direction? Yes, indeed, steps were heard there. They came nearer. A man appeared. He went in the line of the house toward Amanda's balcony; now he walked past a lantern; Mansana saw an officer's cap and a beardless face; he saw Amanda bow lower toward the street. A young girl who loves, actually thinks she sees the beloved object in every place, at all times, and especially one whom she loves in fear. The officer walked more slowly when he descried her; under the balcony he paused and looked up. Amanda hastened into the house and closed the door; the officer walked on.

8

Had they agreed on a trysting-place? Mansana started full run across the square; but the officer had already turned the corner, and when Mansana reached it the officer was no longer in the street. Into which house had he disappeared? It would not do to rouse the whole street to find out; he must give up the search.

By so trifling an incident as that of a young officer, who dwelt in the neighborhood, passing beneath a balcony on which a young damsel was standing alone, — by so trifling an occurrence as this, Mansana's destiny was fulfilled.

He went to bed that night, not to sleep, but to vow to himself over and over again, in the anguish of his heart, that the next morning she should be his, or he would not live.

But the next morning she was not on the heights. He waited an hour and still no one came. Then he went to her house. Before the door to the lodgings of the Brandinis stood an old woman, with their breakfast and a note. As Mansana was about to seize the knocker, the old woman said, " There is no one at home here, as it seems. But read this note that was hanging on the knocker." Mansana took it. " Gone away. More later. B." He let the note fall and strode away. The old woman

called after him to ask what was in the note.
But he made no reply.

Princess Leaney, on reaching Ancona the
next day and not meeting Mansana on the
platform, experienced great anxiety ; she knew
not why. She went herself to the telegraph
office and sent him hearty greetings, which
plainly expressed her fear. She then hastened
home and waited ; her alarm grew with every
hour. Finally the telegram was returned
with the money that had been paid for the
reply message. Captain Mansana had left the
town.

Terror overpowered her. The self-reproaches
in which she had daily lived became mountains ;
they shut out every prospect. She must go
where he was, find him, talk with him, tend
him ; she suspected the worst. Evening found
her at the railway station, accompanied by a
single servant.

In the dawn of the morning the next day she
was walking back and forth at the junction
with the road from the west. There were not
many travelers at the station, and those who
were there she did not see. All the more did
they look at her as she swept past them, back
and forth, wrapped in a white fur cloak which

she had so thrown over her shoulders that the arms hung loose, and with a fur cap on her head, beneath which her floating hair and veil had become entangled. The large eyes and the whole face evinced emotion and weariness. In her restless walk she often passed by a tall lady, plainly clad, who stood gazing intently at the luggage-van, where several men were busied. Another time when the princess passed, there appeared an officer who addressed the lady, and to a question from the luggage-van answered, —

" Mansana."

The princess rushed toward him.

" Mansana ? " cried she.

" Princess Leaney ? " whispered the officer in astonishment, as he bowed to her.

" Major Sardi ! " she said, in reply, adding, hastily : " Mansana ! Did you mention Mansana ? "

" Yes, this is his mother."

As he introduced them, the mother drew her veil aside, and there was such power in her face to arouse the confidence of the princess that the latter threw herself into her arms as into a sure refuge from all sorrowing thoughts, and then she burst into passionate tears. Mansana's mother silently embraced her, but stood as one who was waiting. She patted her affectionately but said nothing.

When Theresa could command words she asked, —

" Where is he ? "

" None of us know," replied the mother, calmly.

" But we hope to know soon," added Sardi.

The princess sprang up, white as chalk, staring at them both.

" What has happened ? " cried she.

The thoughtful mother, who had braved so many storms, said quietly, —

" We have doubtless the same journey before us. Let us take a compartment to ourselves, and then we can talk matters over and hold counsel together."

This was done.

CHAPTER XIII.

THE Brandini family had gone to the home of Nina Borghi, Brandini's sister and Luigi's mother. It so chanced that on the same night train by which the Brandinis fled, the hero

Luigi also took flight. They discovered one another at a station late the next morning, as
Luigi was about to leave the train. He was so
alarmed that he would have pushed past them
without speaking; but old Brandini held fast
to him and poured into his ear his tale of woe.
Luigi merely said, —

"Go to mother," and hastened away.

He went, however, to the telegraph office
immediately on reaching his garrison, and, in a
very excited frame of mind, telegraphed to his
mother announcing her brother's approach.
The telegram was couched in such anxious
words that the lady to whom it was addressed,
and who lived alone outside of Castellamare,
near Naples, became much alarmed. She was
not less so when her brother and his daughter
arrived and told her what threatened both them
and her son.

Captain Mansana had conjectured that the
Brandinis had gone south, for there was no
night train on any but the southern route. He
followed. But after vainly seeking during two
days a starting-point for further investigations,
he turned about and directed his course toward
the town where Luigi Borghi was stationed.
He must know where the two were, and this
knowledge he should impart to him or take the

consequences! As Mansana was aware that
he was well known in the town, he went to
work with great caution, in order that Luigi
might have no warning. Consequently he was
obliged to pass two days in the town before he
met him. This occurred on the street, when
Mansana had been searching for him in one of
the little cafés of the townspeople. To his astonishment, Luigi was not frightened, as he had
expected to find him. And to his still greater
astonishment, Luigi unhesitatingly told where
the Brandini family were. Mansana became
suspicious. He called Luigi's attention to what
it would cost to speak anything but the truth,
but the little officer did not even blink as he
swore that what he said was true.

Further settlement with the lieutenant must
be postponed. That same day Mansana took
the train south.

What did he want? Uncompromisingly the
same: she should be his! This was why Luigi
had been so leniently treated. Since Amanda's
warily undertaken flight, there was a tempest
raging within Mansana's soul; no one should
venture to treat him thus unpunished. He did
not love her; no, he hated her, and that was
why she should he his! If not!— This brief
train of thought kept revolving round and round

in his mind. The air was filled with confused
pictures of his comrades standing in groups
laughing at him. He certainly had been made
a fool of by a little girl just out of a convent,
and a little lieutenant just out of school!

How it had come so far that this conflict with
two insignificant children should be the end of
his proud career, he could not make clear to
himself.

Princess Leaney's image — which during his
first excitement rarely rose up before him and
was angrily thrust aside when it did appear —
kept growing clearer and clearer the more exhausted and ashamed he became. She was
the goal of the life for which he was destined,
so lofty was his aim! And he thought no
longer of her rank, but of the glowing course of
her thoughts, of the beauty of her presence, ex-
alted by the admiration of all mortals.

Amanda's image sank away at the same time.
He was not sure but that she was round-shoul-
dered. He was actually able to speculate upon
this.

People who have made us ridiculous in our
own eyes and those of others are not very apt
to be the gainers thereby. And when Mansana had reached the point where he could dis-
cover that Amanda's figure was awkward, her

face and conversation insignificant, her voice drawling, her hair absurdly arranged, her flattery much too soft and insinuating, he asked himself if it would not be the most ludicrous thing in the world to compel such a person to become Signora Mansana. No, there was something that would be still more absurd, and that was to kill himself for her sake.

What should he do, then? Go back to the princess? That path was barred — barred by his pride a hundred thousand times! *Past* Amanda and onward, to the Spanish civil war, for instance? An adventurer's career, hollow, empty! Just as well end his life at home.

Turn back and let all be as before? The princess lost, the admiration of his comrades lost, faith in himself lost! The only way in which he could return was at her side, that cursed little woman! With her by the hand he could appear as victor, and if he must pay for this prize with an unhappy life, so it must be. His honor would then be saved, and no one should be allowed to read his soul.

There would be actual glory in having rejected a wealthy princess, and captured the daughter of a poor pensioned officer, in a conflict even with herself! But the moment he reached this conclusion, his soul revolted at all the deception which such an honor as this must contain. He sprang up from his seat in the compartment, but sat down again; — there were several passengers within.

The train proceeded onward toward his goal. What a goal! Ruin was inevitable, his life must surely be sacrificed to honor; and this whether honor was attained or no.

The merciful power of sleep intervened. He dreamed of his mother. Her large, noble eyes hung over him like a heaven. He wept and was awakened. There was an old man in the compartment who was deeply affected by his tears. Just then the train stopped. They were in the vicinity of Naples; Mansana got out. The morning was glorious. The clear sky, bordered by the faint outlines of the chain of hills, served as a reminder and a warning; he shivered in the chill morning air and returned to the smoke of the locomotive which was just starting, to the rumbling and din of the train as it stormed onward, and to his own stinging thoughts.

Farther on, as they passed along the seashore, he would have given much if the train had deviated from its course and slowly and smoothly glided out into the trackless waters. What gentle deliverance in such a death!

He hid himself in his corner when the train stopped at Naples; in the vast human throng about the station there might be some one who knew him. The day became more and more glorious while the train glided through the coast towns along the sea; the sun was mild as on a summer morning, and its rays in the hazy sea atmosphere cast a tinge over mountain, sea, and the entire landscape. When he got out of the compartment and was driving toward his destination, and still more after he had dismissed the carriage and was climbing the steep cliffs, with the sea at his feet and the grand view over the gulf, bordered with islands that looked like shapeless sea-monsters on guard, and with mountains under the dominion of Vesuvius and towns gleaming white beneath a slow smoke, then he felt a sense of life — not his *own life* which was but a chase after honor, a struggle, he knew not himself for what, *now* that this struggle had ended in absolutely nothing — no, life as it was meant to be beneath God's high arching heavens, in the splendor of *His* glory which overspread all nature and thus extended beyond the goal which life usually marks out.

He approached the last hill, on which the house he was seeking was situated. Soon he saw the house, which stood beyond the summit of the hill, surrounded by a high, sharp-pointed iron fence. Then his heart began to throb. There could be no mistake ; he had, moreover, taken the route accurately pointed out by the coachman.

So this was the place! And before his feelings were clear to his own mind, she appeared on the balcony, she, Amanda, in her bright morning gown, with a smile on her lips, as if she had said or heard something amusing as she stepped out. She saw him at once, uttered her well-known scream and ran in.

As a weary huntsman when suddenly brought face to face with his game regains all his elasticity, so Mansana felt rising within him a wild power, an untamed purpose, and before he knew what he was about, he stood at the gate of the iron fence and had bounded over it without ringing the bell. Controlled by his own lively emotions, all his warrior-like instincts were aroused ; he turned at once and possessed himself of the key which was on the inner side of the gate. The door to the house was half closed ; he pushed it open. He was admitted to a large, bright vestibule. Colored glass cast its own peculiar play over some small statues, a mosaic inlaid stone floor and vases, filled with palms, fan-palms, and flowers. On a pair of antique sofas were lying, on one a straw hat with blue ribbons — was it hers? — on the other a parasol of a peculiar watered material with a costly carved handle whose end was studded with a large blue stone. He recognized it, and a wounded feeling followed the recollections evoked, but he made no effort to explain this. For now he rang the bell. He must make haste.

No one came to open the door. He began to shiver, then tried to control himself, but failed. He could not remain longer thus. If he could not execute his purpose at once he was lost. He rang once more. His will rose with the act. Now it was necessary to make or break. The door to the room opened, a bright light flooded the vestibule ; the stained glass did not permit him to see more than that the person who was approaching and who closed the door behind her was blue and tall. As soon as the door was closed all became dark in the hall. Who could it be ? Might not the house chance to be filled with people? An actual terror seized him at this thought, which had not occurred to him a moment before. What mad pranks, what complications, what interferences, and inconvenient persons might not here assail him! He was perhaps entering a bee-hive of provoked anger and resistance; it might prove to be a fool's errand he was on! *No, on such an errand he would not go a second time!* And he put on the whole armor of his will, and made sure that his weapon was by him. Then the large door was thrown wide open, and before him in the lofty doorway —

Yes, there in the lofty doorway stood Theresa Leaney, clad in blue, and very pale.

And he? He stood there motionless, his self-possession gone.

The door was wide open; they stood on either side of the threshold. Silent as themselves was all within and without. At last she extended her right hand. There ran a tremor through his frame; she stretched out both arms; he rushed into her ready embrace with a ring like that of an instrument which has been struck. And he took her up in his arms, bore her out to the sofa, sat down with her on his lap, plunged his head against her bosom, and clasping her in a warm embrace, rose up with her in his arms, sat down again and broke into the most vehement flood of tears on her bosom. Not a word of explanation!

He finally put her down beside him on the sofa and flung himself on his knees. He gazed with boundless admiration into her smiling face. Now he was overcome, conquered; never in the world would it have been well with Giuseppe Mansana had it not been so.

And when, in burning gratitude, he raised his eyes, purified by this feeling of humility, it was not hers they met; they fell on another behind him — there stood his mother.

Both he and Theresa arose. Instinctively he sought his mother's hands. When he held them in his own he kissed them, and once more falling on his knees guided them to his head. What had he not experienced since he had so defiantly met her gaze beside his father's bier.

Mansana never got beyond the entrance of this house. The two ladies went back to say farewell; he preceded them down the hill. Why precede them? Because he wanted to put a key quietly in the gate, and because he wished, in all haste and shame, to fling a revolver into the sea. These things accomplished, he sank down on a stone, overwhelmed with fear, joy, gratitude, dismay, — all inextricably blended. The two who followed him, accompanied by a servant with their luggage, saw him sitting below the road, with his head in his hands. They walked together to the railway station.

He did not need to hear much in order to understand how this meeting had come about. It was Sardi who had summoned them; they had sought Luigi Borghi in hopes that *he* would be informed about the Brandinis, and that Mansana would sooner or later find his way to them. That was why Luigi had been so courageously frank, because he knew the two ladies to be already at his mother's house.

Mansana had relapsed into silence.

The wise mother had a foreboding of danger, and begged for rest at Naples, declaring that she needed it herself. They went to a quiet suburban hotel. Here, after much resistance, Mansana's mother got him to bed. And when at last he slept, it seemed as though he would never again awaken. Almost the whole of the next day passed. When he did awake he found himself alone; he was confused and became alarmed, but a few trifles in the room reminded him of his mother and Theresa; he laid back again and slept like a happy child. This time, however, he did not sleep as long as before, for hunger awoke him. He ate, but fell asleep again. For several days and nights he slept, almost without interruption. But when he rose from his couch he was very quiet. He retired more and more into brooding silence.

This was just what his mother had anticipated.

CHAPTER XIV.

THE end shall be told by a letter from Theresa Leaney to Mansana's mother. It was dated from the writer's estate in Hungary, not long after the events last related.

BELOVED MOTHER, — At last you shall have a connected account of everything since we parted at Naples. If I repeat anything that I have written before you must pardon me.

Well, then, after our marriage his illness gave place to an eager, humble zeal in serving me, which made me anxious, for it was so unlike him. Upon the whole he was neither confiding nor self-reliant, until after we had been in the town where he was last stationed. He understood perfectly why you wished us to go there first. Ah, how amiable he was there ! He began forthwith to run the gauntlet among his comrades, I may say in the most dauntless

9

manner. I can tell you, furthermore, about a
young wife who aided him. She had never
been happier or more elegant, you see, than
when she became the companion of her noble
husband in his humiliation; every movement,
every expression of her face, every word,
seemed, as it were, freighted with " If *I* say
nothing, who *then* dare say a word ? "

I am, alas, still so much of a coquette that I
have a great desire to inform you how I was
dressed each of these three days. (I had sent
to Ancona for my maid and my wardrobe.)
But I will meekly hold my peace.

I am perfectly sure, though, that dearly as a
certain young wife was loved after those three
days' running the gauntlet in this mountain
town, not many women have been loved; for
there is power in the temperament you yourself
have given from your own soul, you delightful
being.

Nor must I forget to sound the praises of
the man Sardi. For he *is* a man. He had done
such a good thing, in announcing that Mansana was ill, — which he truly was, — and that
you and I were his physicians. The good fortune of it all is that he who has won fame
among his comrades has also laid up in their
hearts treasures on which he may draw for a

long time before they are exhausted. People *will* think well of Giuseppe Mansana. He felt this, the dear man, and it made him very humble ; for he was sorely oppressed by the thought that he did not deserve it.

In Ancona everything went smoothly ; the stubbornness of his nature was conquered. And now he is all mine, — mine the strongest nature in the world, purified and ennobled, — mine the most considerate of masters, the most attentive of servants, — mine the most manly lover that ever Italian girl won. Pardon my strong expressions ; I know you do not like them, but they *must* come.

At Bologna — aye, you see I fly — we were walking about and chanced to pass the municipal building. There hang two marble tablets bearing the names of those who fell in the struggle for the town's freedom. Giuseppe's arm trembled, and to this circumstance it was due that we had a conversation than which nothing could form a surer foundation for our union.

You know, beloved mother, how my eyes were opened during the time when I was grieving over the wrong I had done Giuseppe through my despicable caprices, which nearly cost him his life and both of us our happiness. You know that my soul is daily racked with indignation against those public affairs that breed in us defiance, hatred, frenzied fanaticism, culpable intolerance. Unwholesome, unnatural public affairs poison a community and do more harm than the most miserable open warfare ; for there is no possibility of estimating how much spiritual strength they consume, how many hearts they bereave, how many homes they lay waste! I assure you, mother, that a land which, for instance, has made an unjust conquest, captured what belongs to others, transforms a whole community into sharers of its guilt, lowers the general moral standard, sharpens the pen of the strategist, the crow-bar of the burglar, the harsh words of the commander — ah! it drives the heart from its rights in the family and in society !

There are some stupid verses that were written about me by an enamored fool; not one word in them is true. But do you know, dearest mother, I feel now that had I not met Giuseppe, those lines might one day have become true, for stupid and heartless as they are I would finally have become equally stupid and heartless! And why so ? Because the unhappy state of public affairs had strewed poison into my existence.

And my confessions were brought face to face with Giuseppe's. That defiant, vain will of his had so entirely become his master that the most trifling and chance interference might easily have cost him his life, the most accidental aim have changed his course. But this defiant, vain will, — in what atmosphere was it bred ?

We gave each other the most complete confidence, that evening at Bologna. And then for the first time everything seemed so secure ; ah, so secure !

Here, on my dearly loved estate he has now set to work. All was chaos here, and he has something now on which he can exercise his will ! He wishes to resign ; he is determined to .be no longer a peace officer. He needs a fixed goal, and one that is close at hand ; if I divine rightly it is the one which lies hidden from the world that is dearest to him.

Thus, at all events, matters stand for the present. What later developments may arise I know not. But I do know that if ever Italy be in danger, he will be one of the first — and that in all respects.

God bless you! Come up here soon. You must see him in his busy life, and you must see him with me. Has ever mortal at any time

had so considerate a husband, so noble a lover?
Ah, I forgot — my extravagant expressions are
not allowed, and yet I assure you they are the
only ones I can use!

I love you, I long to embrace you again and
again, and kiss you, beloved mother of my joy!

Darling, sorely - tried woman, from whose
eyes go forth a song of praise, from whose lips
words of consolation and help fall so refresh-
ingly! You, aye you, must bow your white
head in prayer over our happiness, that it may
be blessed! Listen! You must be our teacher
that the evil days may not come too soon.

Your son's wife, your own, your faithful
THERESA.

THE RAILROAD AND THE CHURCHYARD.

CHAPTER I.

KNUD AAKRE belonged to an old family in the parish, where it had always been renowned for its intelligence and its devotion to the public welfare. His father had worked his way up to the priesthood, but had died early, and as the widow came from a peasant stock, the children were brought up as peasants. Knud had, therefore, received only the education afforded by the public schools of his day; but his father's library had early inspired him with a love of knowledge. This was further stimulated by his friend Henrik Wergeland, who frequently visited him, sent him books, seeds, and much valuable counsel. Following some of the latter, Knud early founded a club, which in the beginning had a very miscellaneous object, for instance: " to give the members prac-

tice in debating and to study the constitution,"
but which later was turned into a practical
agricultural society for the entire bailiwick.
According to Wergeland's advice, he also
founded a parish library, giving his father's
books as its first endowment. A suggestion
from the same quarter led him to start a Sunday-
school on his gard, for those who might wish to
learn writing, arithmetic, and history. All this
drew attention to him, so that he was elected
member of the parish board of supervisors, of
which he soon became chairman. In this ca-
pacity, he took a deep interest in the schools,
which he brought into a remarkably good condition.

Knud Aakre was a short man, brisk in his
movements, with small, restless eyes and very
disorderly hair. He had large lips, which were
in constant motion, and a row of splendid teeth
which always seemed to be working with them,
for they glistened while his words were snapped
out, crisp and clear, crackling like sparks from
a great fire.

Foremost among the many he had helped to
gain an education was his neighbor Lars Högstad. Lars was not much younger than Knud,
but he had developed more slowly. Knud
liked to talk about what he read and thought,

and he found in Lars, whose manner was quiet
and grave, a good listener, who by degrees
grew to be a man of excellent judgment.   The
relations between them soon became such that
Knud was never willing to take any important step without first consulting Lars Högstad, and the matter on hand was thus likely
to gain some practical amendment.   So Knud
drew his neighbor into the board of supervisors,
and gradually into everything in which he himself took part.   They always drove together
to the meetings of the board, where Lars never
spoke ; but on the way back and forth Knud
learned his opinions.   The two were looked
upon as inseparable.

One fine autumn day the board of supervisors
convened to consider, among other things, a
proposal from the bailiff to sell the parish grain
magazine and with the proceeds establish a
small savings-bank.   Knud Aakre, the chairman, would undoubtedly have approved this
measure had he relied on his unbiased judgment.   But he was prejudiced, partly because
the proposal came from the bailiff, whom Wergeland did not like, and who was consequently
no favorite of Knud's either, and partly because the grain magazine had been built by his

influential paternal grandfather and by him presented to the parish. Indeed, Knud was rather inclined to view the proposition as a personal insult, therefore he had not spoken of it to any one, not even to Lars, and the latter never entered on a topic that had not first been set afloat by some one else.

As chairman, Knud Aakre read the proposal without adding any comments; but, as was his wont, his eyes sought Lars, who usually sat or stood a little aside, holding a straw between his teeth, — he always had one when he took part in a conversation; he either used it as a tooth-pick, or he let it hang loosely in one corner of his mouth, turning it more rapidly or more slowly, according to the mood he was in. To his surprise Knud saw that the straw was moving very fast.

"Do you think we should agree to this?" he asked, quickly.

Lars answered, dryly, —

"Yes, I do."

The whole board, feeling that Knud held quite a different opinion, looked in astonishment at Lars, but the latter said no more, nor was he further questioned. Knud turned to another matter, as though nothing had transpired. Not until the close of the meeting did he resume the subject, and then asked, with apparent indifference, if it would not be well to send the proposal back to the bailiff for further consideration, as it certainly did not meet the views of the people, for the parish valued the grain magazine. No one replied. Knud asked whether he should enter the resolution in the register, the measure did not seem to be a wise one.

" Against one vote," added Lars.

" Against two," cried another, promptly.

" Against three," came from a third ; and before the chairman could realize what was taking place, a majority had voted in favor of the proposal.

Knud was so surprised that he forgot to offer any opposition. He recorded the proceedings and read, in a low voice : " The measure is recommended, — adjourned."

His face was fiery red as he rose and put up the minute-book ; but he determined to bring forward the question once more at the meeting of the representatives. Out in the yard, he put his horse to the wagon, and Lars came and took his seat at his side. They discussed various topics on their way home, but not the one they had nearest at heart.

The next day Knud's wife sought Lars's wife to inquire if there was anything wrong between

the two men, for Knud had acted so strangely
when he came home. A short distance above
the gard buildings she met Lars's wife, who was
on her way to ask the same question, for her
husband, too, had been out of sorts the day before. Lars's wife was a quiet, bashful person,
somewhat cowed, not by harsh words, but by
silence, for Lars never spoke to her unless she
had done something amiss, or he feared that
she might do wrong. Knud Aakre's wife, on the
other hand, talked more with her husband, and
particularly about the board, for lately it had
taken his thoughts, work, and affection away
from her and the children. She was as jealous
of it as of a woman ; she wept at night over the
board and quarreled with her husband about
it during the day. But for that very reason
she could say nothing about it now when for
once he had returned home unhappy ; for she
immediately became more wretched than he,
and for her life she could not rest until she had
discovered what was the matter. Consequently,
when Lars's wife could not give her the desired
information, she had to go out in the parish to
seek it. Here she obtained it, and of course
was at once of her husband's opinion ; she found
Lars incomprehensible, not to say wicked.
When, however, she let her husband perceive

this, she felt that as yet there was no breach
between Lars and him ; that, on the contrary,
he clung warmly to him.

The representatives met. Lars Högstad drove
over to Aakre in the morning ; Knud came out
of the house and took his seat beside him.
They exchanged the usual greetings, spoke
perhaps rather less than was their wont on the
way, and not of the proposal. All the members of the board were present; some, too, had
found their way in as spectators, which Knud
did not like, for it showed that there was a
stir in town about the matter. Lars was armed
with his straw, and he stood by the stove warming himself, for the autumn was beginning to
be cold. The chairman read the proposal, in a
subdued, cautious manner, remarking when he
was through, that it must be remembered this
came from the bailiff, who was not apt to be
very felicitous in his propositions. The building, it was well known, was a gift, and it is not
customary to part with gifts, least of all when
there is no need of doing so.

Lars, who never before had spoken at the
meetings, now took the floor, to the astonishment of all. His voice trembled, but whether
it did so out of regard for Knud, or from anxiety
lest his own cause should be lost, shall remain

unsaid. But his arguments were good and
clear, and full of a logic and confidence which
had scarcely been heard at these meetings before. And when he had gone over all the
ground, he added, in conclusion : —

"What does it matter if the proposal does
come from the bailiff? This affects the question as little as who erected the building, or in
what way it came into the public possession."

Knud Aakre had grown very red in the face
(he blushed easily), and he shifted uneasily
from side to side, as was his wont when he was
impatient, but none the less did he exert himself to be circumspect and to speak in a low
voice. There were savings-banks enough in the
country, he thought, and quite near at hand,
he might almost say *too* near. But if, after all,
it was deemed expedient to have one, there
were surely other ways of reaching it than those
leading over the gifts of the dead and the love
of the living. His voice was a little unsteady
when he said this, but quickly recovered as he
proceeded to speak of the grain magazine in itself, and to show what its advantages were.

Lars answered him thoroughly on the last
point, and then added, —

"However, one thing and another lead me to
doubt whether this parish is managed for the

sake of the living or the dead ; furthermore, whether it is the love and hatred of a single family which controls matters here, or the good of the whole."

Knud answered quickly, —

" I do not know whether he who has just spoken has been least benefited by this family, — both by the dead and by him who now lives."

The first shot was aimed at the fact that Knud's powerful grandfather had saved the gard for Lars's paternal grandfather, when the latter, on his part, was absent on a little excursion to the penitentiary.

The straw which long had been in brisk motion, suddenly became still.

" It is not my way to keep talking everywhere about myself and my family," said Lars, then turned again with calm superiority to the subject under discussion, briefly reviewing all the points with one definite object.   Knud had to admit to himself that he had never viewed the matter from such a broad standpoint ; involuntarily he raised his eyes and looked at Lars, who stood before him, tall, heavily built, with clearness on the vigorous brow and in the deep eyes.   The lips were tightly compressed, the straw still played in the corner of his mouth ; all the surrounding lines indicated vigor. He kept his hands behind him, and stood rigidly erect, while his voice was as deep and as hollow as if it proceeded from the depths of the earth. For the first time in his life Knud saw him as he was, and in his inmost soul he was afraid of him ; for this man must always have been his superior. He had taken all Knud himself knew and could impart ; he had rejected the tares and retained what had produced this strong, hidden growth.

He had been fostered and loved by Knud, but had now become a giant who hated Knud deeply, terribly. Knud could not explain to himself why, but as he looked at Lars he instinctively felt this to be so, and all else becoming swallowed up in this thought he started up, exclaiming, —

"But Lars! Lars! what in Heaven's name is the matter with you?" His agitation overcame him, — "you, whom I have — you who have" —

Powerless to utter another word, he sat down ; but in his effort to gain the mastery over the emotion he deemed Lars unworthy of seeing, he brought his fist down with violence on the table, while his eyes flashed beneath his stiff, disorderly hair, which always hung over them. Lars acted as if he had not been interrupted, and turning toward the others he asked if this was to be the decisive blow; for if such were the case there was no need for further remarks.

This calmness was more than Knud could endure.

"What is it that has come among us?" cried he. "We who have, until to-day, been actuated by love and zeal alone, are now stirred up against each other, as though goaded on by some evil spirit," and he cast a fiery glance at Lars, who replied, —

"It must be you yourself who bring in this spirit, Knud; for I have kept strictly to the matter before us. But you never can see the advantage of anything you do not want yourself; now we shall learn what becomes of the love and the zeal when once this matter is decided as we wish."

"Have I then illy served the interests of the parish?"

There was no reply. This grieved Knud, and he continued, —

"I really did persuade myself that I had accomplished various things — various things which have been of advantage to the parish; but perhaps I have deceived myself."

10

He was again overcome by his feelings ; for his was a fiery nature, ever variable in its moods, and the breach with Lars pained him so deeply that he could scarcely control himself. Lars answered, —

" Yes, I know you appropriate the credit for all that is done here, and if one should judge by the amount of speaking at these meetings, you certainly have accomplished the most."

" Is that the way of it ? " shouted Knud, looking sharply at Lars. " It is you who deserve the entire honor ? "

" Since we must finally talk about ourselves," said Lars, " I am free to admit that every question has been carefully considered by both of us before it was introduced here."

Here little Knud Aakre regained his ready speech : —

" Take the honor, in God's name ; I am quite able to live without it ; there are other things that are harder to lose ! "

Involuntarily Lars evaded his gaze, but said, as he set the straw in very rapid motion, —

" If I were to express *my* opinion, I should say that there is not very much to take credit for. No doubt the priest and the school-masters are content with what has been done ; but certainly the common people say that up to the present time the taxes of this parish have grown heavier and heavier."

Here arose a murmur in the crowd, and the people grew very restless. Lars continued, —

" Finally, to-day we have a matter brought before us that might make the parish some little amends for all it has paid out ; this is perhaps the reason why it encounters such opposition. This is a question which concerns the parish ; it is for the welfare of all ; it is our duty to protect it from becoming a mere family matter."

People exchanged glances, and spoke in half-audible tones ; one of them remarked, as he rose to go for his dinner-pail, that these were the truest words he had heard in these meetings for many years. Now all rose from their seats, the conversation became general, and Knud Aakre, who alone remained sitting, felt that all was lost, fearfully lost, and made no further effort to save it. The truth was, he possessed something of the temperament attributed to Frenchmen : he was very good at a first, second, or even third attack, but poor at self-defense, for his sensibilities overwhelmed his thoughts.

He was unable to comprehend this, nor could he sit still any longer, and so resigning his place to the vice-chairman, he left. The others could not refrain from a smile.

He had come to the meeting in company with Lars, but went home alone, although the way was long. It was a cold autumn day, the forest was jagged and bare, the meadow gray-yellow, frost was beginning here and there to remain on the road-side. Disappointment is a terrible companion. Knud felt so small, so desolate, as he walked along; but Lars appeared everywhere before him, towering up to the sky, in the dusk of the evening, like a giant. It vexed him to think it was his own fault that this had been the decisive battle; he had staked too much on one single little issue. But surprise, pain, anger, had mastered him; they still burned, tingled, moaned, and stormed within him. He heard the rumbling of cart-wheels behind him; it was Lars driving his superb horse past him, in a brisk trot, making the hard road resound like distant thunder. Knud watched the broad-shouldered form that sat erect in the cart, while the horse, eager for home, sped onward, without any effort on the part of Lars, who merely gave him a loose rein. It was but a picture of this man's power: he was driving onward to the goal! Knud felt himself cast out of his cart, to stagger on alone in the chill autumn air.

In his home at Aakre Knud's wife was waiting for him. She knew that a battle was inevitble; she had never in her life trusted Lars, and now she was positively afraid of him. It had been no comfort to her that he and her husband had driven away together; it would not have consoled her had they returned in the same way. But darkness had fallen and they had not come. She stood in the doorway, gazing out on the road in front of the house; she walked down the hill and back again, but no cart appeared.

Finally she hears a rattling on the hard road, her heart throbs as the wheels go round, she clings to the casement, peering out into the night; the cart draws near; only one is in it; she recognizes Lars, who sees and recognizes her, but drives past without stopping. Now she became thoroughly alarmed. Her limbs gave way under her, she tottered in and sank down on the bench by the window. The children gathered anxiously about her, the youngest one asked for papa; she never spoke with them but of him. He had such a noble disposition, and this was what made her love him; but now his heart was not with his family, it was engrossed in all sorts of business which brought him only unhappiness, and consequently they were all unhappy.

If only no misfortune had befallen him ! Knud was so hot-tempered. Why had Lars come home alone? Why did he not stop? Should she run after him, or down the road after her husband? She was in an agony of distress, and the children pressed around her, ask· ing what was the matter. But this she would not tell them, so rising she said they must eat supper alone, then got everything ready and helped them. All the while she kept glancing out on the road. He did not come. She un- dressed the children and put them to bed, and the youngest repeated the evening prayer while she bowed over him. She herself prayed with such fervor in the words which the infant lips so soothingly uttered that she did not heed the steps outside.

Knud stood upon the threshold, gazing at his little company at prayer. The mother drew herself up ; all the children shouted : " Papa ! " but he seated himself at once, and said, softly :

" Oh, let him say it once more ! "

The mother turned again to the bedside, that he, meanwhile, should not see her face, for it would have seemed like intruding on his grief before he felt the need of revealing it. The little one folded its hands over its breast, all the rest did likewise, and it repeated, —

"I, a little child, pray Heaven
  That my sins may be forgiven,
  With time I 'll larger, wiser grow,
  And my father and mother joy shall know,
  If only Thou, dearest, dearest Lord,
  Will help me to keep Thy precious word!
  And now to our Heavenly Father's merciful keeping
  Our souls let us trust while we 're sleeping."

What peace now fell upon the room! Not a minute had elapsed ere all the children were sleeping as in the arms of God; but the mother moved softly away and placed supper before the father, who was, however, unable to eat. But after he had gone to bed, he said, —

"Henceforth I shall be at home."

And his wife lay at his side trembling with joy which she dared not betray; and she thanked God for all that had happened, for whatever it might be it had resulted in good!

CHAPTER II.

In the course of a year Lars had become chairman of the parish board of supervisors, president of the savings-bank, and leading commissioner in the court of reconciliation; in short, he held every office to which his election had been possible. In the board of supervisors for

the amt (county) he was silent during the first
year, but the second year he created the same
sensation when he spoke as in the parish board;
for here, too, coming forward in opposition to
him who had previously been the guiding
power, he became victorious over the entire
rank and file and was from that time himself
the leader. From this his path led him to the
storthing (parliament), where his fame had
preceded him, and where consequently there
was no lack of challenges. But here, although
steady and firm, he always remained retiring.
He did not care for power except where he was
well known, nor would he endanger his leader-
ship at home by a possible defeat abroad.

For he had a pleasant life at home. When
he stood by the church wall on Sundays, and
the congregation walked slowly past, saluting
him and stealing side glances at him, and one
after another paused in order to exchange a
few words with him, — then truly it might be
said that he controlled the entire parish with a
straw, for of course this hung in the corner of
his mouth.

He deserved his honors. The road leading
to the church, he had opened; the new church
they were standing beside, he had built; this
and much more was the fruit of the savings-

bank which he had founded and now managed himself. For its resources were further made fruitful, and the parish was constantly held up as an example to all others of self-management and good order.

Knud Aakre had entirely withdrawn from the field, although at first he attended a few of the meetings of the board, because he had promised himself that he would continue to offer his services, even if it were not altogether pleasing to his pride. In the first proposal he had made, he became so greatly perplexed by Lars, who insisted upon having it represented in all its details, that, somewhat hurt, he said: "When Columbus discovered America he did not have it divided into parishes and deaneries ; this came gradually ; " whereupon Lars, in his reply, compared the discovery of America with Knud's proposal, — it so happened that this treated of stable improvements, — and afterwards Knud was known by no other name in the board than "Discovery of America." So Knud thought that as his usefulness had ceased, so too had his obligations to work, and he refused to accept further reëlections.

But he continued to be industrious ; and in order that he might still have a field for usefulness, he enlarged his Sunday-school, and

placed it, by means of small contributions from
the attendants, in communication with the
mission cause, of which he soon became the
centre and leader in his own and the surrounding counties. Thereupon Lars Högstad remarked, that if ever Knud undertook to collect
money for any purpose, he must know beforehand that it was to do good thousands of miles
from home.

There was, be it observed, no more' strife
between them. To be sure, they no longer
associated with each other, but they bowed and
spoke when they met. Knud always felt a
little pain at the mere thought of Lars, but
strove to suppress it, and persuade himself
that matters could not have been otherwise.
At a large wedding-party, many years afterward, where both were present and both were
in good spirits, Knud mounted a chair and proposed a toast for the chairman of the parish
board, and the first representative their amt
had sent to the storthing! He spoke until
he became deeply moved, and, as usual, expressed himself in an exceedingly handsome
way. Every one thought it was honorably
done, and Lars came up to him, and his gaze
was unsteady as he said that for much of what
he knew and was he was indebted to him.

At the next election of the board of supervisors Knud was again made chairman !

But had Lars Högstad foreseen what now
followed, he would certainly not have used his
influence for this. "Every event happens in its
own time," says an old proverb, and just as
Knud Aakre again entered the board, the best
men of the parish were threatened with ruin,
as the result of a speculation craze which had
long been raging, but which now first began to
demand its victims. It was said that Lars Högstad was the cause of this great disaster, for he
had taught the parish to speculate. This penny
fever had originated in the parish board of
supervisors, for the board itself was the greatest speculator of all. Every one down to the
laboring youth of twenty years desired in his
transactions to make ten dollars out of one; a
beginning of extreme avarice in the efforts to
hoard, was followed by an excessive extrava-
gance, and as all minds were bent only on money, there had at the same time developed a
spirit of suspicion, of intolerance, of caviling,
which resulted in lawsuits and hatred. This
also was due to the example of the board, it
was said, for among the first things Lars had
done as chairman was to sue the venerable old
priest for holding doubtful titles. The priest

had lost, but had also immediately resigned. At that time some had praised, some censured this suit; but it had proved a bad example. Now came the consequences of Lars's management, in the form of loss to every single man of property in the parish, consequently public opinion underwent a sharp change! The opposing force, too, soon found a leader, for Knud Aakre had come into the board, introduced there by Lars himself!

The struggle began forthwith. All those youths to whom Knud in his time had given instructions, were now grown up and were the most enlightened men in the parish, thoroughly at home in all its transactions and public affairs. It was against these men that Lars now had to contend, and they had borne him a grudge from their childhood up. When of an evening after one of these stormy proceedings he stood on the steps in front of his house, gazing over the parish, he could hear a sound as of distant rumbling thunder rising toward him from the large gards, now lying in the storm. He knew that the day they met their ruin, the savings-bank and himself would be overthrown, and all his long efforts would culminate in imprecations heaped on his head.

In these days of conflict and despair, a party

of railroad commissioners, who were to survey the route for a new road, made their appearance one evening at Högstad, the first gard at the entrance to the parish. In the course of conversation during the evening, Lars learned that there was a question whether the road should run through this valley or another parallel to it.

Like a flash of lightning it darted through his mind that if he could succeed in having it laid here, all property would rise in value, and not only would he himself be saved but his fame would be transmitted to the latest posterity! He could not sleep that night, for his eyes were dazzled by a glowing light, and sometimes he could even hear the sound of the cars. The next day he went himself with the commissioners while they examined the locality; his horse took them, and to his gard they returned. The next day they drove through the other valley; he was still with them, and he drove them back again to his house. They found a brilliant illumination at Högstad; the first men of the parish had been invited to be present at a magnificent party given in honor of the commissioners; it lasted until morning. But to no avail, for the nearer they came to a final issue, the more plainly it appeared that the road could not pass through this locality without undue expense. The entrance to the valley lay through a narrow gorge, and just as it swung into the parish, the swollen river swung in also, so that the railroad would either have to take the same curve along the mountain that the highway now made, thus running at a needlessly high altitude and crossing the river twice, or it would have to run straight forward, and thus through the old, now unused churchyard. Now the church had but recently been removed, and it was not long since the last burial had taken place there.

If it only depended on a bit of old churchyard, thought Lars, whether or not this great blessing came into the parish, then he must use his name and his energy for the removal of this obstacle ! He at once set forth on a visit to the priest and the dean, and furthermore to the diocese council; he talked and he negotiated, for he was armed with all possible facts concerning the immense advantage of the railroad on one hand, and the sentiments of the parish on the other, and actually succeeded in winning all parties. It was promised him that by a removal of part of the bodies to the new churchyard the objections might be considered set aside, and the royal permission obtained for the churchyard to be taken for the line of railroad. It was told him that nothing was now needed but for him to set the question afloat in the board of supervisors.

The parish had grown as excited as himself : the spirit of speculation which for many years had been the only one prevailing in the parish, now became madly jubilant. There was nothing spoken or thought of but Lars's journey and its possible results. When he returned with the most magnificent promises, they made much of him ; songs were sung in his praise ; indeed, if at that time the largest gards had gone to destruction, one after another, no one would have paid the slightest attention to it : the speculation craze had given way to the railroad craze.

The board of supervisors assembled : there was presented for approval a respectful petition, that the old churchyard might be appropriated as the route of the railroad. This was unanimously adopted ; there was even mention of giving Lars a vote of thanks and a coffee-pot in the form of a locomotive. But it was finally thought best to wait until the whole plan was carried into execution. The petition came back from the diocese council, with a demand for a list of all bodies that would have to be removed. The priest made out such a list, but instead of sending it direct, he had his own reasons for sending it through the parish board. One of the members carried it to the next meeting. Here it fell to the lot of Lars, as chairman, to open the envelope and read the list.

Now it chanced that the first body to be disinterred was that of Lars's own grandfather! A little shudder ran through the assembly! Lars himself was startled, but nevertheless continued to read. Then it furthermore chanced that the second body was that of Knud Aakre's grandfather, for these two men had died within a short time of each other. Knud Aakre sprang from his seat; Lars paused; every one looked up in consternation, for old Knud Aakre had been the benefactor of the parish and its best beloved man, time out of mind. There was a dead silence, which lasted for some minutes. At last Lars cleared his throat and went on reading. But the further he proceeded the worse the matter grew; for the nearer they came to their own time, the dearer were the dead. When he had finished, Knud Aakre asked quietly whether the others did not agree with him in thinking that the air about them was filled with spirits. It was just beginning to grow dark in the room, and although they were mature men and were sitting in numbers together, they could not refrain from feeling alarmed. Lars produced a bundle of matches from his pocket and struck a light, dryly remarking, that this was no more than they knew beforehand.

" Yes, it is," said Knud pacing the floor, " it is more than I knew before. Now I begin to think that even railroads can be purchased too dearly."

These words sent a quiver through the audience, and observing that they had better further consider the matter, Knud made a motion to that effect.

" In the excitement which had prevailed," he said, " the benefit likely to be derived from the road had been overestimated. Even if the railroad did not pass through this parish, there would have to be stations at both ends of the valley ; true, it would always be a little more troublesome to drive to them than to a station right in our midst ; yet the difficulty would not be so very great that it would be necessary because of it to violate the repose of the dead."

Knud was one of those who when his thoughts were once in rapid motion could present the most convincing arguments ; a moment before what he now said had not occurred to his mind, nevertheless it struck home to all.

11

Lars felt the danger of his position, and con-
cluding that it was best to be cautious, apparently acquiesced in Knud's proposition to
reconsider. Such emotions are always worse
in the beginning, he thought; it is wisest to
temporize with them.

But he had miscalculated. In ever increasing waves the dread of touching the dead of
their own families swept over the inhabitants
of the parish ; what none of them had thought
of as long as the matter existed merely in the
abstract, now became a serious question when it
was brought home to themselves. The women
especially were excited, and the road near the
court-house was black with people the day of
the next meeting. It was a warm summer day,
the windows were removed, and there were as
many without the house as within. All felt
that a great battle was about to be fought.

Lars came driving up with his handsome
horse, and was greeted by all; he looked calmly
and confidently around, not seeming to be surprised at anything. He took a seat near the
window, found his straw, and a suspicion of a
smile played over his keen face as he saw Knud
Aakre rise to his feet to act as spokesman for
all the dead in the old Högstad churchyard.

But Knud Aakre did not begin with the

churchyard. He began with an accurate exposition of how greatly the profits likely to accrue from having the railroad run through the parish had been overestimated in all this turmoil. He had positive proofs for every statement he made, for he had calculated the distance of each gard from the nearest station, and finally he asked, —

"Why has there been so much ado about this railroad, if not in behalf of the parish?"

This he could easily explain to them. There were those who had occasioned so great a disturbance that a still greater one was required to conceal it. Moreover, there were those who in the first outburst of excitement could sell their gards and belongings to strangers who were foolish enough to purchase. It was a shameful speculation which not only the living but the dead must serve to promote!

The effect of his address was very considerable. But Lars had once for all resolved to preserve his composure let come what would. He replied, therefore, with a smile, that he had been under the impression that Knud himself was eager for the railroad, and certainly no one would accuse him of having any knowledge of speculation. (Here followed a little laugh.) Knud had not evinced the slightest objection to

the removal of the bodies of common people for
the sake of the railroad; but when his own
grandfather's body was in question then it suddenly affected the welfare of the whole community! He said no more, but looked with a
faint smile at Knud, as did also several others.
Meanwhile, Knud Aakre surprised both him
and them by replying: —

"I confess it; I did not comprehend the
matter until it touched my own family feelings; it is possible that this may be a shame,
but it would have been a far greater one not
to have realized it at last — as is the case with
Lars! Never," he concluded, "could this rail-
lery have been more out of place; for to people with common decency the whole affair is
absolutely revolting."

"This feeling is something that has come up
quite recently," replied Lars, "we may therefore hope that it will soon pass over again.
May it not perhaps help the matter a little to
think what the priest, dean, diocese council, en-
gineers, and government will all say if we first
unanimously set the ball in motion, then come
and beg to have it stopped? If we first are
jubilant and sing songs, then weep and deliver
funeral orations? If they do not say that we
have gone mad in this parish, they must at all

events say that we have acted rather strangely
of late."

"Yes, God knows, they may well think so!"
replied Knud. "We have, indeed, acted very
strangely of late, and it is high time for us to
mend our ways. Things have come to a serious
pass when we can each disinter his own grandfather to make way for a railroad; when we
can disturb the resting-place of the dead in
order that our own burdens may the more
easily be carried. For is not this rooting in our
churchyard in order to make it yield us food
the same thing? What is buried there in the
name of Jesus, we take up in Moloch's name
— this is but little better than eating the bones
of our ancestors."

"Such is the course of nature," said Lars,
dryly.

"Yes, of plants and of animals."

"And are not we animals?"

"We are, but also the children of the living
God, who have buried our dead in faith in
Him: it is He who shall rouse them and not
we."

"Oh, you are talking idly! Are we not
obliged to have the graves dug up at any rate,
when their turn comes? What harm is there
in having it happen a few years earlier?"

"I will tell you. What was born of them still draws the breath of life; what they built up yet remains; what they loved, taught, and suffered for, lives about us and within us; and should we not allow them to rest in peace?"

"Your warmth shows me that you are thinking of your own grandfather again," replied Lars, "and I must say it seems to me high time the parish should be rid of *him*. He monopolized too much space while he lived; and so it is scarcely worth while to have him lie in the way now that he is dead. Should his corpse prevent a blessing to this parish that would extend through a hundred generations, we may truly say that of all who have been born here, *he* has done us the greatest harm."

Knud Aakre tossed back his disorderly hair, his eyes flashed, his whole person looked like a bent steel spring.

"How much of a blessing what you are speaking about may be, I have already shown. It has the same character as all the other blessings with which you have supplied the parish, namely, a doubtful one. It is true, you have provided us with a new church, but you have also filled it with a new spirit, — and it is not that of love. True, you have furnished us with new roads, but also with new roads to destruction, as is now plainly manifest in the misfortunes of many. True, you have diminished our public taxes, but you have increased our private ones ; lawsuits, promissory notes, and bankruptcies are no fruitful gifts to a community. And *you* dare dishonor in his grave the man whom the whole parish blesses ? You dare assert that he lies in our way ; aye, no doubt he does lie in your way, this is plain enough now, for his grave will be the cause of your downfall ! The spirit which has reigned over you, and until to-day over us all, was not born to rule but to enter into servitude. The churchyard will surely be allowed to remain in peace ; but to-day it shall have one grave added to it, namely, that of your popularity which is now to be buried there."

Lars Högstad rose, white as a sheet ; his lips parted, but he was unable to utter a word, and the straw fell. After three or four vain efforts to find it again and recover his powers of speech, he burst forth like a volcano with, —

" And so these are the thanks I get for all my toil and drudgery ! If such a woman-preacher is to be allowed to rule — why, then, may the devil be your chairman if ever I set my foot here again ! I have kept things together until this day, and after me your trash will fall into a thousand pieces, but let it tumble down now — here is the register!" And he flung it on the table. "Shame on such an assembly of old women and brats!" Here he struck the table with great violence. "Shame on the whole parish that it can see a man rewarded as I am now."

He brought down his fist once more with such force that the great court-house table shook, and the inkstand with its entire contents tumbled to the floor, marking for all future generations the spot where Lars Högstad fell in spite of all his prudence, his long rule, and his patience.

He rushed to the door and in a few moments had left the place. The entire assembly remained motionless; for the might of his voice and of his wrath had frightened them, until Knud Aakre, remembering the taunt he had received at the time of *his* fall, with beaming countenance and imitating Lars's voice, exclaimed : —

"Is *this* to be the decisive blow in the matter?"

The whole assembly burst into peals of merriment at these words! The solemn meeting ended in laughter, talk, and high glee; only a few left the place, those remaining behind called for drink to add to their food, and a night of thunder succeeded a day of lightning. Every one felt as happy and independent as of yore, ere the commanding spirit of Lars had cowed their souls into dumb obedience. They drank toasts to their freedom; they sang, indeed, finally they danced, Knud Aakre and the vice-chairman taking the lead and all the rest following, while boys and girls joined in, and the young folks outside shouted "Hurrah!" for such a jollification they had never before seen!

CHAPTER III.

LARS moved about in the large rooms at Hög-stad, without speaking a word. His wife, who loved him, but always in fear and trembling, dared not come into his presence. The management of the gard and of the house might be carried on as best it could, while on the other hand there kept growing a multitude of letters, which passed back and forth between Högstad and the parish, and Högstad and the post-office; for Lars had claims against the parish board, and these not being satisfied he prosecuted;

against the savings-bank, which were also un-satisfied, and so resulted in another suit. He took offense at expressions in the letters he received and went to law again, now against the chairman of the parish board, now against the president of the savings-bank. At the same time there were dreadful articles in the news-papers, which report attributed to him, and which were the cause of great dissension in the parish, inciting neighbor against neighbor Sometimes he was absent whole weeks, no one knew where, and when he returned he lived as secluded as before. At church he had not been seen after the great scene at the representa-tives' meeting.

Then one Saturday evening the priest brought tidings that the railroad was to run through the parish after all, and across the old church-yard! It struck like lightning into every home. The unanimous opposition of the par-ish board had been in vain, Lars Högstad's influence had been stronger. This was the meaning of his journeys, this was his work! Involuntary admiration of the man and his stubborn persistence tended to suppress the dissatisfaction of the people at their own defeat, and the more they discussed the matter the more reconciled they became; for a fact accom-

plished always contains within itself reasons
why it is so, which gradually force themselves
upon us after there is no longer possibility
of change. The people assembled about the
church the next day, and they could not help
laughing as they met one another. And just
as the whole congregation, young and old, men
and women, aye, even children, were all talking
about Lars Högstad, his ability, his rigorous
will, his immense influence, he himself with
his whole household came driving up in four
conveyances, one after the other. It was two
years since his last visit there ! He alighted
and passed through the crowd, while all, as by
one impulse, unhesitatingly greeted him, but he
did not deign to bestow a glance on either side,
nor to return a single salutation. His little
wife, pale as death, followed him. Inside of
the church, the astonishment grew to such a
pitch that as one after another caught sight of
him they stopped singing and only stared at
him. Knud Aakre, who sat in his pew in front
of Lars, noticed that there was something the
matter, and as he perceived nothing remarkable
in front of him, he turned round. He saw Lars
bowed over his hymn-book, searching for the
place.

He had not seen him since that evening at

the meeting, and such a complete change he
had not believed possible. For this was no
victor! The thin, soft hair was thinner than
ever, the face was haggard and emaciated, the
eyes hollow and bloodshot, the giant neck had
dwindled into wrinkles and cords. Knud comprehended at a glance what this man had gone
through; he was seized with a feeling of strong
sympathy, indeed, he felt something of the old
love stirring within his breast. He prayed for
Lars to his God, and made a resolute vow that
he would seek him after service; but Lars had
started on ahead. Knud resolved to call on
him that evening. His wife, however, held him
back.

"Lars is one of those," said she, " who can
scarcely bear a debt of gratitude : keep away
from him until he has an opportunity to do
you some favor, and then perhaps he will come
to you ! "

But he did not come. He appeared now and
then at church, but nowhere else, and he associated with no one. On the other hand, he
now devoted himself to his gard and other business with the passionate zeal of one who had
determined to make amends in one year for the
neglect of many ; and, indeed, there were those
who said that this was imperative.

Railroad operations in the valley began very soon. As the line was to go directly past Lars's gard, he tore down the portion of his house that faced the road, in order to build a large and handsome balcony, for he was determined that his gard should attract attention. This work was just being done when the temporary rails for the conveyance of gravel and timber to the road were laid and a small locomotive was sent to the spot. It was a beautiful autumn evening that the first gravel car was to pass over the road. Lars stood on his front steps, to hear the first signal and to see the first column of smoke; all the people of the gard were gathered about him. He gazed over the parish, illumined by the setting sun, and he felt that he would be remembered as long as a train should come roaring through this fertile valley. A sense of forgiveness glided into his soul. He looked toward the churchyard, a part of which still remained, with crosses bowed down to the ground, but a part of it was now the railroad. He was just endeavoring to define his own feeling when the first signal whistled, and presently the train came slowly working its way along, attended by a cloud of smoke, mingled with sparks, for the locomotive was fed with pine wood. The wind blew toward the house so that those standing without were soon enveloped in a dense smoke, but as this cleared away Lars saw the train working its way down through the valley like a strong will.

He was content, and entered his house like one who has come from a long day's work. The image of his grandfather stood before him at this moment. This grandfather had raised the family from poverty to prosperity; true, a portion of his honor as a citizen was consumed in the act, but he had advanced nevertheless! His faults were the prevailing ones of his time: they were based on the uncertain boundary lines of the moral conceptions of his day. Every age has its uncertain moral distinctions and its victims to the endeavor to define them properly.

Honor be to him in his grave, for he had suffered and toiled! Peace be with him! It must be good to rest in the end. But he was not allowed to rest because of his grandson's vast ambition; his ashes were thrown up with the stones and the gravel. Nonsense! he would only smile that his grandson's work passed over his head.

Amid thoughts like these Lars had undressed and gone to bed. Once more his grandfather's image glided before him. It was sterner now than the first time. Weariness enfeebles us, and Lars began to reproach himself. But he defended himself also. What did his grandfather want? Surely he ought to be satisfied now, for the family honor was proclaimed in loud tones above his grave. Who else had such a monument? And yet what is this? These two monstrous eyes of fire and this hissing, roaring sound belong no longer to the locomotive, for they turn away from the railroad track. And from the churchyard straight toward the house comes an immense procession. The eyes of fire are his grandfather's, and the long line of followers are all the dead. The train advances steadily toward the gard, roaring, crackling, flashing. The windows blaze in the reflection of the dead men's eyes. Lars made a mighty effort to control himself, for this was a dream, unquestionably but a dream. Only wait until I am awake! There, now I am awake. Come on, poor ghosts!

And lo! they really did come from the churchyard, overthrowing road, rails, locomotive and train, so that these fell with a mighty crash to the ground, and the green sod appeared in their stead, dotted with graves and crosses as before. Like mighty champions they

advanced, and the hymn, "Let the dead repose
in peace!" preceded them.   Lars knew it;
for through all these years it had been sighing
within his soul, and now it had become his re-
quiem; for this was death and death's visions.
The cold sweat started out over his whole body,
for nearer and nearer — and behold, on the
window pane! there they are now, and he
heard some one speak his name.   Overpowered
with dread he struggled to scream; for he was
being strangled, a cold hand was clinching his
throat and he regained his voice in an agonized: "Help me!" and awoke.   The window had been broken in from the outside; the
pieces flew all about his head.   He sprang up.
A man stood at the window, surrounded by
smoke and flames.

"The gard is on fire, Lars! We will help
you out!"

It was Knud Aakre.

When Lars regained his consciousness, he
was lying outside in a bleak wind, which chilled
his limbs.   There was not a soul with him; he
saw the flaming gard to the left; around him
his cattle were grazing and making their voices
heard; the sheep were huddled together in a
frightened flock; the household goods were
scattered about, and when he looked again he

saw some one sitting on a knoll close by, weeping. It was his wife. He called her by name. She started.

"The Lord Jesus be praised that you are alive!" cried she, coming forward and seating herself, or rather throwing herself down in front of him. "O God! O God! We surely have had enough of this railroad now!"

"The railroad?" asked he, but ere the words had escaped his lips, a clear comprehension of the case passed like a shudder over him; for, of course, sparks from the locomotive that had fallen among the shavings of the new side wall had been the cause of the fire. Lars sat there brooding in silence; his wife, not daring to utter another word, began to search for his clothes; for what she had spread over him, as he lay senseless, had fallen off. He accepted her attentions in silence, but as she knelt before him to cover his feet, he laid his hand on her head. Falling forward she buried her face in his lap and wept aloud. There were many who eyed her curiously. But Lars understood her and said, —

"You are the only friend I have."

Even though it had cost the gard to hear these words, it mattered not to her; she felt so happy that she gained courage, and rising up

12

and looking humbly into her husband's face,
she said, —

"Because there is no one else who under-
stands you."

Then a hard heart melted, and tears rolled
down the man's cheeks as he clung to his wife's
hand.

Now he talked to her as to his own soul.
Now too she opened to him her mind. They
also talked about how all this had happened, or
rather he listened while she told about it.
Knud Aakre had been the first to see the fire,
had roused his people, sent the girls out over
his parish, while he had hastened himself with
men and horses to the scene of the conflagra-
tion, where all were sleeping. He had engi-
neered the extinguishing of the flames and the
rescuing of the household goods, and had himself dragged Lars from the burning room, and
carried him to the left side of the house from
where the wind was blowing and had laid him
out here in the churchyard.

And while they were talking of this, some
one came driving rapidly up the road and
turned into the churchyard, where he alighted.
It was Knud, who had been home after his
church-cart, — the one in which they had so
many times ridden together to and from the

meetings of the parish board. Now he requested Lars to get in and ride home with him. They grasped each other by the hand, the one sitting, the other standing.

" Come with me now," said Knud.

Without a word of reply, Lars rose. Side by side they walked to the cart. Lars was helped in ; Knud sat down beside him. What they talked about as they drove along, or afterwards in the little chamber at Aakre, where they remained together until late in the morning, has never been known. But from that day they were inseparable as before.

As soon as misfortune overtakes a man, every one learns what he is worth. And so the parish undertook to rebuild Lars Högstad's houses, and to make them larger and handsomer than any others in the valley. He was reëlected chairman, but with Knud Aakre at his side ; he never again failed to take counsel of Knud's intelligence and heart — and from that day forth nothing went to ruin.

DUST.

CHAPTER I.

THE drive from the town to Skogstad, the large gard belonging to the Atlung family, with its manufacturing establishment on the margin of the woodland stream, at the usual steady pace, might possibly occupy two hours; but in the fine sleighing we had been having it could scarcely take an hour and a half. The road was a chaussé running along the fjord. All the way from town I had the fjord on the right-hand side, and on the left broad fields, gently sloping down from the heights and dotted with villas and gards, surrounded by hedges of trees and having avenues leading to them.

Farther on, the heights became mountains, and rose more abruptly from the shore; here, too, they became more and more rugged, and at last had no other growth than the pine forest, from the uppermost ridge all the way down to the fjord, forest, forest, far as the eye could reach. This belonged to Skogstad; the factory on the Skogstad River prepared the raw material.

The Atlungs were of French descent, having settled here in the times of the Huguenots, and were people of plain origin who had bettered their condition by marrying into the once wealthy and influential Atlung family, taking its name, which sounded not unlike their own.

I thoroughly enjoyed the drive. It had recently been snowing, and the snow still lay on the trees; not a breath of wind had left its traces in the wood. On the other hand, it had been thawing a little, which the deciduous trees that here began to press forward farther down toward the road could not tolerate; the sole covering they wore was the new-fallen snow of the morning.

Between both the white landscape and the snow-laden air, the fjord appeared black. It was not far to the opposite side, and there still loftier mountains loomed up, now also white, but of that subdued tint imparted by the atmosphere.

Where I was driving the sea lay close up to the edge of the snow, only a few sea-weeds,

some pebbles, and in some places not so much
as these, separated the two forms and hues of
the same element — reality and poetry, where
the poetry is just as real as the reality, simply
not so enduring.

As soon as I had advanced as far as the
forest, this attracted my undivided attention.
The fir-trees held great armfuls of snow; in
some places it had been showered around; nevertheless there was still so much uncovered that a
shimmer of dark green overspread the white-
ness of the entire forest.   On a nearer view
it could be seen that the single uncovered
branches were thrust forth, as it were, defiantly,
and that the red-tinted lower boughs had
pierced the snow-drifts.

Higher up mighty trunks were visible, most
of them dark, although some of the younger
ones were brighter: taken all together an assemblage of well-laden giants, and this gave an air
of solemnity to the thicket.   The foremost
trees, which were low enough not to impede the
view, and which while growing had been dis-
figured either by man or beast, perhaps too by
the storms (for they had borne the brunt of
these), had not the regular shapes of the others;
they were more gnarled, affording the snow an
opportunity to commit what ravages it chose

among them. Their lowest branches were in some places quite bowed to the ground, often making the tree appear like an unbroken mass of white ; others were fantastically transformed into clumsy dwarfs, with only upper parts to their bodies, or into sundry human forms, each with a white sack drawn over the head, or a shirt that was not put on right.

Alongside of these awkward figures I noticed small clusters of deciduous trees, over which but the faintest suspicion of snow was spread ; a single one, which stood apart from the rest, looked as though its outmost white branches, as they grew finer and finer, gradually flowed into the air; then there were young spruce trees which formed pyramid upon pyramid of regular layers of snow. Close down by the sea, where there were more stones, might now and then be seen a bramble bush. The snow had spread itself on every thorn, so that the bush looked as if it were strewed over with white berries.

I rounded a naze with a crag upon it, and here is where Skogstad proper begins. The ridge recedes and is broken by the river. Again we see gently sloping fields, and here lies the gard. The river flows farther away ; the red roof and a row of buildings alongside become

visible. On either side of the gard lie the
housemen's places with their surrounding
grounds, but they are separated from the gard
by fields on the one side and by a wood or
park on the other.

At the sight of the park I forgot all that
had gone before. Originally it was intended to
slope down to the sea; but the stony ground
had evidently rendered this impossible, and so
the trees on the lower square had been felled;
but in the course of years, instead of pine woods
a vigorous growth of deciduous trees had shot
up. These, being of the same year's growth,
were of an equal height, and extended all the
way up to the venerable pine trees in the park.
The effect of the delicate encircling the ponder-
ous, the light opposed to the heavy, the low and
perpetually level at the foot of the upward-
soaring and powerful, was very fine.

The eye reveled in this, searching for forms;
I would combine a hundred branches in one
survey, because they ran parallel in the same
curve, at about the same height; or I would
single out one solitary bough from the rest and
follow it from its first ramification through the
branches of its branches to the most delicate
twig, — a distended, transparent white wing,
or a monstrous fern leaf strewed all over with

white down.   Then I was compelled once more to cease following the forms and turn to the colors; the unequal coating presented an infinite variety.

I turned my back on my traveling companion, the fjord, and wound my way up to the gard. Where the park ended, the garden began, and the road followed this in a gradual ascent.   Once there had been a wood here also, and the road had passed through it; but of the wood there was left but a few yards, on either side, thus forming the avenue.   Large, old trees were about being replaced by young ones, whose growth was so dense that in some places I could not see the gard I was driving toward. But the snow-romance followed, decking the sinking giants with white flags, powdering the young and fresh ones, and playing Christmas masquerade with the deformed ones.

CHAPTER II.

THE impressions of nature play their part in our anticipations of what we are about to meet. What was there so white and refined in the experience that awaited me here?

She was not clad in white, to be sure, the last time I saw her, the bright attractive being whom I was now to meet again. On her wedding journey, and in Dresden, some nine years previous to this time, we had last been together. True, she was dressed in gala attire every day — a whim of the young bridegroom, in his blissful intoxication ; but most frequently she wore blue, not once did she appear in white ; nor would it have been becoming to her.

I remember them especially as they sang at the piano, he sitting, because he was playing the accompaniment, she standing and usually with her hand on his shoulder ; but what they sang was indeed white, at least it was always of the character of a more or less jubilant anthem. She was the daughter of a sectarian priest, and they had just come from the parsonage and from the wedding feast. Since then I had heard of them from time to time at the parsonage, and from that source I had received repeatedly renewed urgent entreaties to visit them the next time I was in their vicinity. I was now on my way to them.

I had heard the dwelling-house spoken of as one of the largest frame buildings in Norway. It was gray and immensely long. No Atlung had ever been satisfied with what his predecessor had built, and so the house had had an addition made to it by every generation and a partial remodeling of the old portions, so far as it was necessary to make these correspond with the new. I had heard that many and long passages (concerning which at festal gatherings rhymes without end were said to have been made) endeavor to unite the interior in the same successful or unsuccessful manner as the out-buildings, sloping roof, balconies, and verandas attempt to keep up the style of the exterior. I have heard how many rooms there are in the house, but I have forgotten it.

The last addition was made by the present owner, and is in a sort of modernized gothic style.

Behind the dwelling the other buildings of the gard form a crescent, which, however, protrudes in rather an unsightly manner on one side. Between these and the dwelling I now drove in order to alight, according to the post-boy's advice, at a porch in the gothic wing. I did not see a living being about the gard, not even a dog. I waited a little but in vain, then walked through the porch into a passage, where I took off my wraps, and then passed on into a large bright front room to the right. Neither did I see any one here; but I heard

either two children's voices and a woman's
voice, or two female voices and one child's
voice, and I recognized the song, for it was one
that was just then floating about the country,
the lament of a little girl that she was everywhere in the way except in heaven with God,
who was so glad to have unhappy children with
Him. It sounded rather strange to hear such a
lament in this bright, lively room, filled with
guns and other sporting implements, reindeer
horns, fox skins, lynx skins, and similar substan-
tial objects, arranged with the most exquisite
taste.

I knocked at the door and entered one of the
most charming sitting-rooms I have seen in this
country, so bright its outlook on the fjord, so
large it was, so elegant. The brightly polished
wooden panels of the wall were relieved by
carved wooden brackets, each bearing a bust or
a small statue ; the stylish furniture was in
every direction gracefully distributed about on
the Brussels carpet. Moody and Sankey's
dreamy melody flowed out over this like a
white or yellow sheet. This hymn belongs to a
collection of Christian songs which are among
the most beautiful that I know; but it made the
same impression here as if beneath this modern
room there was a crypt from the Middle Ages

where immured nuns were taking part in ceremonies for the dead, amidst smoking lamps, and whence incense and low chanting, inseparably blended, stole up into the bright conceptions and cheerful art of the nineteenth century.

The singing proceeded from one woman and two boys, the elder of the latter seven years old or a little more, and the younger about six. The woman turned her face toward the door, and paused quite astonished at my entrance; the boys were gazing out of the window, and did not look at her; they were wholly absorbed in their singing, and therefore they continued a while after she had ceased.

Of these two boys the one resembled the father's family, the other the mother's; only the mother's eyes had been bestowed on them both. The elder of the boys had a long face, with high brow and sandy hair, and he was freckled like his father. The younger one had his mother's figure, and stooped slightly because the head was set forward on the shoulders. But in consequence of this his head was usually thrown somewhat backward in order to recover its equilibrium. The result of this again was that the lips were habitually parted, and then the large, questioning eyes and the bright curly

hair encircling the fine arched brow were exactly like the mother's. The elder one was tall
and thin, and had his father's lounging gait and
small, outward turned feet. I observed all this
at a glance, while the boys walked across the
room to the table by the sofa, as their companion
left them. She had advanced, after a moment's
hesitation, to meet me; she was evidently not
sure whether she knew me or not. On hearing
my name, she discovered with a smile that it
was only my portrait she had seen, the portrait
in the album, a souvenir of the wedding journey
of the heads of the house. She informed me
that Atlung was at the factories, and would be
home to dinner, that is to say in about an hour,
and that the mistress of the house was at one
of the housemen's places I had seen from the
road ; it seemed that there was an old man lying at the point of death there.

She made this announcement in a melodious,
although rather feeble voice, and with a pair of
searching eyes fastened on me. She had heard
something about me. I had never thought that
I should see one of Carlo Dolci's madonnas step
down from a frame to stand in a modern sitting-
room and talk with me, and therefore my eyes
were certainly not less searching than hers. The
way the head was poised on the shoulders, its

inclination to one side, the profile of the face,
and beyond all else the eyes and the eyebrows,
indeed, the bluish green head kerchief, which
was drawn far forward, imparting to the pale
face something of its own hue — altogether a
genuine Carlo Dolci !

She walked noiselessly away, and left me
alone with the boys, whom I at once attacked.
The elder one was named Anton, and he could
walk on his hands, at least, almost ; and the
younger one informed me that his name was
Storm, and told me a great deal more about his
brother, whom he regarded with unqualified
admiration. The elder, on the other hand, assured me that his brother Storm was a very
bad boy sometimes ; he had recently been
caught at some of his naughty tricks, and so
papa had given him a flogging that same day ;
Stina had told papa about it. Stina was the
name of her who had just left us.

After this not very diplomatic introduction
to an acquaintance, they stood one on each side
of me and prattled away about what at present was working in their minds, with most extraordinary force. They both now told me,
the elder one taking the lead and the younger
following with supplementary details, that yonder at one of the houseman's places, past which

I had driven, lived Hans, little Hans; that is he
had lived there, for the real, true little Hans
was with God. He had come to the gard to
play with the boys almost every day; though
sometimes they too had been over at the housemen's places, which I soon perceived were to the
boys the promised land of this earth. Then
one evening, about a fortnight since, Hans had
started to go home at dusk; it was before the
snow came, and in the park, through which he
had to pass, the fish pond lay spread before him
so smooth and black. Hans thought he would
like to slide on it and he climbed up from the
path on to the pond, for the path ran right
along it. But that same day there had been a
hole cut in the ice for the people to fish, and
they had forgotten to put a signal there, and so
little Hans slid right into the hole. A child's
cry of distress had reached the gard; the milkmaid had heard it, but only once, and she had
not thought very much about it, for all the boys
were in the habit of playing in the park. So
little Hans had disappeared and no one could
say where he was. Then the ice was cut away
from the pond and they found him; but the
boys were not allowed to see him. They had,
however, been permitted to be present at the funeral with all the little boys and girls of the

factory school. But Hans was not buried in the
chapel where grandfather and grandmother lie ;
he was buried in the churchyard. Oh, what
beautiful singing they had had ! The school-
master had sung bass with them, and the old
brown horse had drawn Hans, who was in a
white painted coffin that papa had bought in
town, and there were garlands of flowers on it.
Mamma and Stina had arranged them. All the
children got cakes before they started and cur-
rant wine. And the song was the one the boys
had just been singing ; Stina had taught it to
them. Hans had been very poor ; but now he
had all he wanted; he was with God ; it was
only the coffin that was put in the ground.
What was in the coffin ? Why, it was not the
real Hans that was there, for Hans was quite
new now. Angels had come down to the pond
with everything that the new Hans was to wear,
so that he did not feel cold in the pond ; he was
not there. All children who died went to God,
and that together with a hundred thousand
million very small angels. The angels were all
round about us here too ; but we could not see
them because they were invisible, and Hans was
now with them. The angels could see us, and
they were so kind to us, especially to children,
and they always wanted to have very unhappy

13

little children with them; that was the reason why they took them. It is ever and ever and ever so much nicer to be with the angels than to be here. Yes, indeed, it is, for Stina said so. Stina too would rather be with the angels than here; it was only for mamma's sake that Stina did not go to them, for mamma would be so lonely without her. All angels had wings, and now Hans's father was lying ill, and he would soon be with Hans. He also would have wings and be a little angel and fly about here and wherever he himself chose — right up to the stars. For the stars were not only stars, they were as large, as large, when we got up to them, as large as the whole earth, and that was enormously large, larger than the largest mountain. And there were people on the stars, and there were many things that were not here. And that same afternoon Hans's father was to go right to God, for God was up in heaven. They would like so much to see Hans's father get his wings; but mamma would not let them go with her. And Hans's father had already become so beautiful, as he lay in his bed, that he almost looked like an angel. Mamma had said so; but they were not allowed to see him.

Stina made her appearance as they came to

the last words; she bade them come with her, and they obeyed.

A door stood open to the left; I could see book-shelves in the room to which it led, so that I presumed the library must be there. I felt a desire to know what the father of these boys was reading just then — provided that he read at all. The first thing I found open on the desk, by the side of letters, account-books, and factory samples, was Bain. And Bain's English friends were the first books my eyes beheld on the nearest shelves. I took out one, and saw that it had been much read. This accorded with what I had heard of Atlung.

Just then bells were heard outside. I thought it must be the mistress of the house returning, and put back the books in the same order I had found them. In so doing I disarranged some behind them (for the books stood in two rows), and I felt a desire to examine also these that were hidden from view, which took time. I did not leave the library until just as the lady was entering the front door.

CHAPTER III.

FRU [1] ATLUNG was evidently glad to see me. She had a singular walk; it seemed as though she never fully bent her knees; but with this peculiar gait she advanced hastily toward me, grasped my hands with both of hers, and looked long into my eyes, until her own filled with tears. It was, of course, the wedding journey this look concerned, the most beautiful days of her life; — but the tears?

Nay, unhappy she could not be. She was so thoroughly the same as she was formerly, that had she not been somewhat plumper, I could not — at all events, not at once — have detected the slightest change. The expression of her countenance was exactly the same innocent, questioning one, not the slightest suggestion of a sterner line or a change of coloring; even the hair fell in the same ringlets about the backward thrown head, and the half parted lips had the same gentle expression, were just as untouched by will, the eyes wore the same look of mild happiness, even the slightly-veiled tone of the voice had the same childlike ring as of yore.

[1] Fru corresponds to the German Frau, and means Mrs.— Translation.

" You look as though you had not had a single new experience since last we met," was the first remark I could not help making to her.

She looked up smiling into my face, and not a shadow contradicted my words. We took our seats, each in a chair that stood out on the carpet, near the library door; our backs were turned to the windows, and thus we faced a wall where between the busts and statues that rested on the carved wooden brackets, there hung an occasional painting on the polished panels.

I gave an account of my trip, received thanks for coming at last. I delivered greetings from her parents, of whom we talked a little. She said she had been thinking of her father to-day, she would have been so glad to have had him with her; for she had just come from a dying man, whose death-bed was the most beautiful she had ever witnessed. Meanwhile, she had assumed her favorite position, that is to say, she sat slightly bowed forward, with her head thrown back, and her eyes fixed on the upper part of the wall, or on the ceiling. As she sat thus, she pressed one finger against her open under lip, not once, but with a constant repetition of the same movement. Now and then the upper portion of her body swayed to and fro.

Her eyes seemed to be fixed; they did not seek my face, either when she asked a question or when she received an answer, unless something special had attracted her from her position. Even then she would promptly resume it.

"Do you believe in immortality?" she asked, as though this were the most natural question in the world, and without looking at me.

But as I was surprised, and consequently compelled to look at her, I perceived that a tear was trickling down her cheek, and that those open eyes of hers were full of tears.

I felt at once that this question was a pretext; it was her husband's belief she was thinking of. Therefore I thought I would spare her further pretexts.

"What is your husband's opinion of immortality?"

"He does not believe in the immortality of the individual," replied she; "we perpetuate ourselves in our intercourse with those about us, in our deeds, and above all in our children: but this immortality, he thinks, is sufficient."

Her eyes were fixed as before, and they were still full of tears; but her voice was mild and calm; not a trace of discontent or reproach in the simple statement, which doubtless was correct.

No, she is not one of the so-called childlike women, I thought; and if she has the same innocent, questioning expression she had nine years ago, it is not because she has been without thought or research.

" You talk, then, with Atlung about these subjects, I suppose ? "

" Not now."

" In Dresden you seemed to be thoroughly united about these things; you sang together "—

" He was under father's influence then. Besides, I think he was not quite clear in his own mind at that time. The change came gradually."

" I saw some books, that are now placed behind the others."

" Yes, Albert has changed."

She sat motionless, as she gave this answer, except that her finger continued its play on the under lip.

" But who, then, attends to the education of the children ? " asked I.

Now she turned half toward me. I thought for a while that she did not intend to answer; but after a long time she did speak.

" No one," said she.

" No one ? "

" Albert prefers to have it so for the present."

"But, my dear lady, if no one teaches them, at least one thing or another is told to them?"

"Yes, there is no objection to that; and it is usually Stina who talks with them."

"And so it is left entirely to chance?"

She had turned from me, and sat in her former attitude.

"Entirely to chance," she replied, in a tone that was almost one of indifference.

I briefly related to her what Stina had told the boys about the life beyond the grave, about angels, etc., and I inquired if she approved of this.

She turned her face toward me. "Yes; why not?" said she. Her great eyes viewed me so innocently; but as I did not answer immediately the blood slowly coursed up into her face.

"If anything of the kind is to be told to them," said she, "it must be something that will take hold of their childish imaginations."

"It confuses the reality for them, my dear lady, and *that* is the same thing as to disturb the development of their faculties."

"Make them stupid, do you mean?"

"Well, if not exactly stupid, it would at least hinder them from using their faculties rightly."

"I do not understand you."

"When you teach children that life here below is nothing to the life above, that to be visible is nothing in comparison to being invisible, that to be a human being is far inferior to being an angel, that to live is not by any means equal to being dead, *is that* the way to teach them to view life properly, or to love life, to gain courage for life, vigor for work, and patriotism?"

"Ah, in that way! Why, *that* is our duty to them later."

"Later, my dear lady? After all this dust has settled upon their souls?"

She turned away from me, assumed her old position, stared fixedly at the ceiling, and became absorbed in thought.

"Why do you use the word dust?" she began presently.

"By the word dust I mean chiefly that which has been, but which now having become disintegrated, floats about and settles in vacant places."

She remained silent a little while.

"I have read of dust which carries the poison from putrified matter. You do not mean that, I suppose?"

There was neither irony nor anger in the

tone, so I failed to understand at what she was aiming.

" That depends on where the dust falls, my dear lady ; in healthy human beings it only creates a cloud of mist, prejudices which prevent them from seeing clearly ; if there be stagnation this dust will oftentimes collect an inch thick, until the machinery is thoroughly clogged."

She turned toward me with more vivacity than she had yet shown, and leaning on the arm of her chair brought her face nearer to mine.

" How did you happen upon this idea ? " asked she. " Is it because you have seen how much dust there is in this house ? "

I admitted that I had seen this.

" And yet the chambermaid and Stina do nothing else but clean away the dust, and I did nothing else either at first. I cannot understand it. At home at my mother's, there was nothing I heard so much about as dust. She was always busied about father with a damp cloth ; he was constantly annoyed because she would disturb his books and papers. But she inisted that he gathered more dust than any one else. He never left his study that she was not after him with a clothes-brush. And later it came to be my turn. I was like my father, she said ;

I accumulated dust, and I never could dust well enough to satisfy her. I was so weary of dust that when I married a Paradise seemed in prospect because I thought I should escape this annoyance and have some one to dust for me. But therein I was greatly in error. And now I have given it up. It is of no use. I evidently have no talent for getting rid of dust."

"And so it is very singular," she continued, as she sank back in her chair, "that you too should come with this talk about dust."

"I hope I have not hurt your feelings?"

"How can you think — ?" and then, in the calmest, most innocent voice in the world, she added: "It would not be easy to hurt the feelings of any one who had lived nine years with Albert."

I became greatly embarrassed. What possible good could it do for me to become entangled in the affairs of this household? I did not say another word. She too sat, or rather reclined in her seat, for a long time in silence, drumming with her fingers on the arms of her chair. Finally I heard, as from far away, the words: "Butterfly dust is very beautiful, though." And then some time afterward there glided forth from the midst of a long chain of thought which she did not reveal, the query, "refracted rays

— the various prismatic colors — ?" She paused, listened, rose to her feet; she had heard Atlung's step in the front room.

I also rose.

CHAPTER IV.

THE door was thrown wide open, and Atlung came lounging in. This tall, slender man, in these capacious clothes that showed many a trace of the factories he had been visiting, bore in his face, his movements, his bearing, the unconcerned ease of several generations.

The gray eyes, beneath the invisible eyebrows, blinked a little when he saw me, and then the long face broadened into a smile. His superb teeth glittered between the full, short lips, as he exclaimed: "Is that you!" He took both my hands between his hard, freckled ones, then dropping one of them threw his arm around his wife's waist. "Was not *that* delightful, Amalie? What? Those days in Dresden, my dear?"

When he had relaxed his hold, he made eager inquiries about myself and my journey, — he knew I was to make a short trip abroad.

Then he began to tell me what occupied *him* the most, and meanwhile he strolled up and down the room, took up one article between his fingers, handled it, then took up another. He did not hold any little thing as others do with the extreme tips of his fingers ; he firmly grasped it in his hand so that his fingers closed over it. In conversation, too, it was just the same : there was a certain fullness in the way he took up each subject and flung it away again at once for something else.

His wife had left the room, but returned very soon and invited us to dinner. Just at that moment Atlung was sauntering past the piano, on which was open a new musical composition, whose character he described in a few words. Then he began to play and sing verse after verse of a long song. When he was through, his wife again reminded him of the meal. This probably first called his attention to her presence in the room.

" See here, Amalie, let us try this duet ! " he cried, and struck up the accompaniment.

Looking at me with a smile, she took her place at his side and joined in the song. Her somewhat veiled, sweet soprano blended with his rich baritone, just as I had heard it nine years before. The voices of both had acquired that deeper, fuller meaning which life gives when it has meaning itself; their skill, on the other hand, was about the same as of old.

Any one who but a moment before might perhaps have found it difficult to understand how these two had come together, only needed to be near them while they sang. A lyric abandonment of feeling was common to both, and where there was any difference of sentiment they were perfectly content to waive it. They floated onward like two children in a boat, leaving the dinner behind them to grow cold, the servants to become impatient, the guest to think what he pleased, and the order of the house and their own plans for the day to be upset.

In their singing there was no energy, no school, no delicate finish of style of this simple number, which, moreover, they were doubtless singing for the first time; but there was a smooth, lazy, happy gliding over the melody. The light coloring of the voices blended together like a caress; and there was a charm in the way it was done

They sang verse after verse, and the longer they continued the better they sang together, and the more joyously. When finally they were through and the wife, with her somewhat labored step, walked into the dining-room on my arm, and Atlung sauntered on before to give Stina the key to the wine-cellar, there was no longer any question in Fru Atlung's eyes, only joy, mild, beautiful joy, and her husband warbled like a canary bird.

We sat down to table while he was still out; we waited an interminable time for him; either he had not found Stina or she had not understood him: he had gone himself to the cellar and had returned so covered with dust and dirt that we could not help laughing. His wife, however, paused in the midst of her laughter, and sat silent while he changed his clothes and washed.

He swallowed spoonful after spoonful of the soup in greedy haste, regained his spirits when his first hunger was satisfied, and began to talk in one unbroken stream, until suddenly, while carving the roast, he inquired for the boys. They had had their dinner; they could not wait so long.

" Have you seen the boys ? " he asked.

" Yes," I replied, and I spoke of their extreme artlessness, and what a strong likeness I thought one bore to his and the other to his wife's family.

" But," he interposed, " it is unfortunate that

both families have comparatively too much imagination; there is an element of weakness in it, and the boys have inherited their share from both families. A very sorrowful occurrence took place here about a fortnight since. A little playfellow was drowned in the fishpond. What the boys have made out of this — of course, with Stina's aid — is positively incredible. I was thinking about it to-day. I have not said anything, for after all it was extremely amusing, and I did not want to spoil their intercourse with Stina. But, indeed, it is most absurd. See here, Amalie, it would almost be better to send them away to school than to let them run wild in this way and get into all kinds of nonsense."

His wife made no reply.

I wanted to divert his attention, and inquired if he had read Spencer's " Essay on Education."

Then he became animated! He had just settled himself to eat, but now he forgot to do so; he took a few bites and forgot again. Indeed, I should judge we sat over this one course a whole hour, while he expatiated on Spencer. That I who had asked if he had read the book in all probability had read it myself, did not trouble him in the least. He gave me a synopsis of the book, often point after point, with his own comments. One of these was that even if, as Spencer desires, pedagogics was introduced into every school, as one of its most important branches — most people would nevertheless lack the ability to bring up their own children ; for teaching is a talent which but few possess. He for his part proposed to send the boys, as soon as they were old enough, to a lady whom he knew to possess this talent and who also had the indispensable knowledge. She was an enthusiastic disciple of Spencer.

He spoke as though this were a matter long since decided upon ; his wife listened as though it were an old decision. I was much surprised that she had not told me of it when we were talking about the children a little while before.

I do not now remember what theme we were drifting into when Atlung suddenly looked at his watch.

" I had entirely forgotten Hartmann ! I should have been in town ! Yes, yes — it is not yet too late ! Excuse me ! "

He threw down his napkin, drank one more glass of wine, rose and left the room. His wife explained apologetically that Hartmann was his attorney ; that unfortunately there was no telegraphic communication between the gard and

14

the town, and that unquestionably there was
some business that must be settled within an
hour or thereabout.

It would take an hour at least to drive to
town, if for nothing else than to spare the
horse; at least an hour there; and then an hour
and a half back, for no one would drive such a
long distance equally fast back and forth with
the same horse. I sat calculating this while I
finished eating, and became aware at the same
time that my coming was most inopportune.
Therefore I resolved that after coffee I too
would take my leave.

We had both finished and now rose from the
table. My hostess excused herself and went
out into the kitchen, and I who was thus left
alone thought I would look round the gard.

When I got out on the steps in front of the
porch, I was met by a burst of loud laughter
from the boys, immediately followed by a word
which I should not have thought they would
take in their mouths, to say nothing of shouting it out with all their might, and this in the
open yard. The elder boy called it out first,
the younger repeated it after him.

They were standing up on the barn bridge,
and the word was addressed to a girl who stood
in the frame shed opposite them, bending over

a sledge. The boys shouted out yet another
word, and still another and another, without
cessation. Between each word came peals of
merriment. It was clear that they were being
prompted by some one inside of the barn door.
The girl made no reply ; but once in a while she
looked up from her work and glanced over her
shoulder — not at the boys but at some one behind the barn where the carriage-shed was
situated.

Then I heard the sound of bells from that direction. Atlung came forth, dressed for his
trip and leading his horse. Great was the alarm
of the boys when they saw their father ! For
they suddenly realized, though perhaps not
distinctly, what they had been shouting, — at
least they felt they had been making mischief
for some one.

"Wait until I get home, boys," the father
shrieked, "and you shall surely both have a
whipping."

He took his seat in his sledge and applied
the lash to his horse. As he drove past me,
he looked at me and shook his head.

The boys stood for a moment as though
turned into stone. Then the elder one took to
his heels with all his strength. The younger
followed, crying, "Wait for me! Say, Anton ;

do not run away from me!" He burst into tears. They disappeared behind the carriage-shed; but for a long time I heard the sobbing of the younger one.

CHAPTER V.

I FELT quite out of spirits, and determined to leave at once; but as I entered the sitting-room my hostess was seated on the large gothic set-tee or sofa, near the dining-room door, and no sooner did she perceive me than she leaned forward across the table in front of her and asked, —

"What do *you* think of Spencer's theory of education? Do you believe we can put it into practice?"

I did not wish to be drawn into an argument, and so merely answered, —

"Your husband's practice, at all events, does not accord with Spencer's teachings."

"My husband's practice? Why, he has none." Here she smiled.

"You mean he takes no interest in the children?"

" Oh, he is like most other men, I suppose,"
she replied; "they amuse themselves with their
children, now and then, and whip them occasionally, too, when anything occurs to annoy
them."

" You believe that husband and wife should
have equal responsibilities in such matters ? "

" Yes, to be sure I do. But even in this respect men have made what division they chose."

I expressed a desire to take my leave. She
appeared much astonished, and asked if I would
not first drink coffee; " but, it is true," she
added, " you have no one to talk with."

She is not the first married woman, I thought,
who makes covert attacks on her husband.

" Fru Atlung ! " I said, " you have no reason
to speak so to me."

" No, I have not. You must excuse me."

It was growing dusk; but unless I was
greatly in error, she was almost ready to weep.

So I took my seat on the other side of the
table. " I have a feeling, dear Fru Atlung,
that you desire to talk to some one ; but I am
surely not the right person."

" And why not ? " she asked.

She sat with both elbows on the table, looking into my face.

" Well, if for no other reason, at least be-

cause such a conversation needs to be entered
into more than once, because there are so many
things to consider, and I am going away again
to-day."

" But cannot you come again ? "

" Do you wish it ? "

She was silent a moment, then she said
slowly : "As a rule, I have but one great wish
at a time. And it was fully in keeping with
the one I now have that *you* should come
here."

" What is it, my dear lady ? "

" Ah, that I cannot tell you, unless you will
promise me to come again."

" Well, then, I will promise you to do so."

She extended her hand across the table with
the words : " Thank you."

I turned on my chair toward her, and took
her hand.

" What is it, my dear lady ? "

" No, not now," she replied ; " but when you
come again. You must help me — if you believe it to be right to do so."

" Of course."

" Because you, I know, think in many par-
ticulars as Atlung does. He will listen to *you*."

" Do you think so ? "

" He will not listen to me, at all events."

" Did you ever make an effort to be heard ? "

" No, that would be the worst thing I could do. With Atlung everything must come as by chance."

" But, dear me ! I noticed that on the whole you seemed to hold most blessed relations with each other."

" Yes, to be sure we do ! We often amuse ourselves exceedingly well together."

I had a feeling that she did not wish me to look at her, and I had turned away, so that I sat with my side to the table as before. The twilight deepened about us.

" You remember us, I dare say, as we were in Dresden ? "

" Yes."

" We were two young people who were play-ing with life ; it had been very amusing to be engaged, but to be married must be still more diverting, and then to come home and keep house, oh ! so immensely entertaining; but not equal to having children. Well, here I am now with a house which I am utterly powerless to manage, and two children which neither of us can educate ; at least Atlung thinks so."

" But do not you try to take hold ? "

" Of the house, do you mean ? "

" Well, yes, of the house."

"Dear me! of what use would that be? I usually get a scolding when I try."

"But you have plenty of help, I suppose?"

"Yes, that is just the misfortune."

I was about to ask what she meant by this when the dining-room door was noiselessly opened; Stina entered with the lamps. She passed in and out two or three times; but the large room was far from being lighted by the lamps she brought in. Meanwhile, conversation ceased.

When Stina was about to leave, Fru Atlung asked for the children. Stina informed her they were being searched for; they were not on the gard. The mother paid no further attention to this, and Stina left the room.

"Who is Stina?" I asked, as the door closed behind her.

"Oh, she is a very unhappy person. She had a drunken father who beat her, and afterwards she had a husband, a bank cashier, who also became a hard drinker and beat her. Now he is dead."

"Has she been here long?"

"Since before my first child was born."

"But this is sad company for you, my dear lady."

"Yes, she is not *very* enlivening."

" Then most surely she should be sent away."

" That would be contrary to the traditions of this house. An older person must always take charge of the children, and this older person must live and die in the family. Stina is a very worthy woman."

Again the subject of our conversation came noiselessly into the room ; this time with the coffee. There was upon the whole something ghost-like about this blue-green Carlo Dolci portrait flitting thus over the rugs in the large room, where she was searching for a shade for the lamp on the coffee table, as though it were not dark enough here before. The shade was, moreover, a perforated picture of St. Peter's at Rome.

Stina departed, and the lady of the house poured out the coffee.

" And so you men are going to take from us the hope in immortality, with all the rest? " she abruptly asked.

To what this " all the rest " referred, I was allowed to form my own conjectures. She handed me a cup of coffee and continued, —

" When I was driving this morning to the other side of the park to visit the dying man, it occurred to me that the snow on the barren trees is, upon the whole, the most exquisite symbol that could be imagined of the hope of immortality spread over the earth; is it not so? So purely from above, and so merciful!"

"Do you believe it falls from the skies, my dear lady?"

"It certainly falls down on the earth."

"That is true, but it comes also from the earth."

She appeared not to want to hear this, but continued, —

"You spoke a little while ago of dust. But this white, pure dust on the frozen boughs and on the gray earth is truly like the poetry of eternity; so it seems to me," and she placed a singing emphasis on the "me."

"Who is the author of this poetry, my dear lady?"

She turned on me her large eyes, now larger than ever, but this time not questioningly; no, there was certainty in her look.

"If there is no revelation from without, there is one from within; every human being who feels thus possesses it."

She had never been more beautiful. At this moment steps were heard in the front room. She turned her head in a listening attitude.

"It is Atlung back again!" said she, as she rose and rang for another cup.

She was right ; it was Atlung, who as soon as
he had removed his out-door wraps opened wide
the door and came in. His attorney, Hartmann,
had grown anxious and had come to meet him.
Atlung had attended to the entire business with
him on the highway.

His wife's questioning eyes followed him as
he sauntered across the floor. Either she did
not like his having interrupted us, or she noticed that he was out of humor. As he took
the coffee cup from her hand, he recounted to
her his recent experience with the boys. He
did not mention any of the words the little fellows had shouted out with such jubilant merriment; but he added enough to lead her to
surmise what they were. And while he was
drinking his coffee, he repeated to her that he
had promised them a whipping ; " but," said
he, " something more than the rod is needed in
this case."

As she stood when she handed him the cup,
so she remained standing after he had finished
his coffee and gone. Terror was depicted in
both face and attitude. Her eyes followed him
as he walked about the room ; she was waiting
to hear this something else which was more
than the rod.

" Now I will tell you what it is, Amalie,"

came from across the room, "the boys must leave to-morrow at latest."

She sank slowly down on the sofa, so slowly that I do not think she was aware that she was seating herself. She watched him intently. A more helpless, unhappy object I had never seen.

"You surely think enough of the boys, Amalie, to submit? You see now the result of my humoring you the last time."

But if he goes on thus he will kill her! Why does he not look at her?

Whether she noticed my sympathy or not, she suddenly turned her eyes, her hands, toward me, while her husband walked from us across the floor; there was a despairing entreaty in this glance, in this little movement. I comprehended at once what was her sole wish: this was the matter in which I was to help her.

She had sunk down on her hands, and she remained lying thus without stirring. I did not hear sounds of weeping; probably she was praying. He strode up and down the room; he saw her; but his step kept continually growing firmer. The articles he picked up and crushed in his hand, he flung each time farther and farther away from him, and with increased vehemence.

The dining-room door slowly opened. Stina

appeared again; but this time she remained standing on the threshold, paler than usual. Atlung, who had just turned toward us, stood still and cried: " What is it, Stina ? "

She did not reply at once; she looked at the mistress of the house, who had raised her head and was staring at her, and who at last burst out : " What is it, Stina ? "

" The boys," said Stina, and paused.

" The boys ? " repeated both parents, Atlung standing motionless, his wife springing up.

" They are neither on the gard, nor at the housemen's places; we have searched everywhere, even through the manufactory."

" Where did you see them last ? " asked Atlung, breathless.

" The milkmaid says she saw them running toward the park crying, when you promised to give them a whipping."

" The fish-pond ! " escaped my lips before I had time to reflect, and the effect upon myself, and upon all the others, was the same as if something had been dashed to pieces in our midst.

" Stina ! " shouted Atlung, — it was not a reproach, no, it was a cry of pain, the bitterest I have ever heard, — and out he rushed. His wife ran after him, calling him by name.

" Send for lanterns ! " I cried to the people
I saw behind Stina in the dining-room. I went
out and found my things, and returning again,
met Stina, who was moving round in a circle
with clasped hands.

" Come now," said I, " and show me the
way ! "

Without reply, perhaps without being conscious of what she was doing, she changed her
march from round in a circle to forward, with
hands still clasped, and praying aloud : " Father in heaven, for Christ's sake ! Father in
heaven, for Christ's sake ! " in touching, vigorous tones ; and thus she continued through
the yard, past the houses, through the garden,
and into the park.

It was not very cold ; it was snowing. As
one in a dream, I walked through the snow-
mist, following this tall, dark spectre in front
of me, with its trail of prayer, in and out
among the lofty, snow-covered trees. I said to
myself that two small boys might of course go
to the fish-pond in the hope of finding God and
the angels and new clothes ; but to spring into
a hole if there was one, when there were two of
them together — impossible, unnatural, absurd !
How in all the world had I come to think of or
suggest such a thing ? But all the sensible

things one can say to one's self at such a moment are of no avail ; the worst and most im-
probable suppositions keep gaining force in
spite of them ; and this " Father in heaven, for
Christ's sake ! Father in heaven, for Christ's
sake ! " which soughed about me, in tones of
the utmost anguish, kept continually increasing
my own anxiety.

Even if the boys had not gone to the fish-
pond, or if they had been there and had not
dared jump into the water, they might have
tumbled into some other place. The father of
little Hans was to receive wings that afternoon ;
might not they, with their troubled hearts, be
sitting under a tree somewhere waiting for
wings to be given them ? If such were the
case, they would freeze to death. And I could
see these two little frozen mortals, who dared
not go home, the younger one crying, the elder
one finally crying too. I positively seemed to
hear them — " Hush ! "

" What is that ? " said Stina, and turned in
sudden hope. " Do you hear them ? "

We both stood still ; but there was nothing
to hear except my own panting when I could
no longer hold my breath. Nor was there anything resembling two little human beings huddled together.

I told her what I had just been thinking
about, and drawing near me she clasped her
hands, and, in tones of suppressed anguish,
whispered : " Pray with me ! Oh, pray with
me ! "

" What shall I pray for ? That the boys
may die, and go to heaven and become angels ? "

She stared at me in alarm, then turned and
walked on as before, but now without a word.

We followed a foot-path through the wood :
it led to the fish-pond, as I remembered from
the story about little Hans ; but we had to go
more than half the length of the park in order
to reach the latter. Through a ravine flowed a
brook, and here a dam had been made. It was
large so that the fish-pond had a considerable
circumference. We had to step up from the
foot-path in order to reach the edge of the
pond. Stina continued to walk in front of me,
and when she had climbed the bank and could
see the pond and the two parents standing on
it, she kneeled down, praying and sobbing.
Now I was sorry for her.

When I also stood upon the bank and saw
the parents, I was deeply affected. At the
same time I heard voices in the wood behind
me. They came from the people with the
lanterns. The flickering light of the four lan-

terns that, subdued by the falling snow, was
shed over human beings, the snow itself, the
lower trunks of the trees, and the shadows into
which some individuals in the party and some
of the trees and certain portions of the landscape occasionally fell, all became fixed forever
in my memory with the words I at that moment
heard from the pond: "There is no hole in the
ice!"

It was Atlung's voice, quivering with emotion. I turned and saw his wife on his neck.
Stina had sprung up with an exclamation which
ended in a long but hushed: "God be praised
and thanked!"

But the two on the ice still clung together;
with some difficulty I climbed down from the
bank and crossed to where they stood; the wife
still hung on Atlung's neck and he was bowed
over her. I paused reverently at a little distance; they were whispering together. The
light shed by the lanterns on the pond was the
first thing that roused them.

"But what next? Where shall we seek
now?" asked Atlung.

I drew nearer. I now repeated to the parents, although more cautiously, what I had already said to Stina, that perhaps the children
were sitting somewhere under a tree, waiting

15

in their distress of mind for compassionate angels, and in that case there would be danger
of their being already so cold that they would
be ill. Before I had finished speaking, Atlung
had called up to those on the bank: "Had the
boys their out-door things on when they were
last seen?"

"No," replied two of the by-standers.

He inquired if they had their caps on; and
here opinions differed. I insisted that they did
have them on; some one else said No. Atlung himself could not remember. Finally some
one declared that the elder boy had his cap on,
but not the younger one.

"Ah, my poor little Storm!" wailed the
mother.

Among the people on the edge of the pond
there were some who wept so loud that they
were heard below. I think there were about
twenty people, side by side, about the lanterns.

Atlung shouted up to them: "We must
search the whole park through; we will begin
with the housemen's places. And he came toward the bank, climbed up and helped his wife
up after him.

They were met by Stina. "My dear, dear
lady!" she whispered, beseechingly; but neither of the parents paid any attention to her.

I stared into the ravine below us. To look down on snow-laden trees from above is like gazing on a petrified forest.

"Dear Atlung! will not you call?" begged the wife.

He took a position far in advance of the rest; all became still. And then he called aloud through the wood, slowly and distinctly : "Anton and little Storm! Come home to papa and mamma! Papa is no longer angry!"

Was it the air thus set in motion, or did the last flake of snow needed to break an over-laden branch fall just then, or had some one come into contact with such a branch; suffice it to say, Atlung received for an answer the snow-fall from a large bough, partly at one side, partly in front of us. It gave a hollow crash, rousing the echoes of the wood, the bough swayed to and fro, and rose to its place, and snow was showered over us. But this swaying motion finally caused all the heavy branches to loose their burdens; crash followed crash, and snow enveloped us; before we knew what was coming the nearest tree had cast the burden from all its branches at once. The atmospheric pressure now became so great that two more, then five, six, ten, twenty trees freed them-selves, with violent din, from their heavy loads,

sending an echo through the wood and a mist
as from mighty snow-drifts. This was followed
by cluster after cluster of trees, some at our
sides, some at a long distance off, some right in
front of us; the movement first passed through
two great arms, which gradually spread into
manifold divisions; ere long the whole forest
trembled. The thunder rolled far away from
us, close by us, now at intervals, now all at once,
and seemed interminable. Before us everything
was surrounded by a white mist; this loud
rumbling of thunder through the wood had at
first appalled us; gradually as it passed farther
on and grew in proportion it became so majes-
tic that we forgot all else.

The trees stood once more proudly erect, fresh
and green; we ourselves looked like snow-men.
All the lanterns were extinguished, we lighted
them again, and we shook the snow from us.
Then we heard in a moaning tone: " What if
the little boys are lying under a snow-drift ! "

It was the mother who spoke. Several hastened to say that it could not in any way harm
them, that the worst possible result would be
that they might be thrown down, perhaps
stifled for a little while; but they would surely
be able to work their way out again. There
was one who said that unquestionably the chil-

dren would scream as soon as they were free from the snow, and Atlung called out: "Hark!" We stood for more than a minute listening; but we heard nothing except a far-off echo from some solitary cluster of trees that had just been drawn into the vortex with the rest.

But if the boys were in one of the remote recesses of the wood, their voices could scarcely reach us; on either side of us the edges of the ravine were higher than the banks of the pond where we stood.

"Yes, let us go search for them," said Atlung, deeply moved; as he spoke, he went close to the brink of the pond, turned toward the rest of us who were beginning to step down, and bade us pause. Then he cried: "Anton and little Storm! Come home again to papa and mamma! Papa is no longer angry!" It was heart-rending to hear him. No answer came. We waited a long time. No answer.

Despondently he returned, and came down on the path with the rest of us; his wife took his arm.

CHAPTER VI.

WE reached the edge of the wood, and then our party divided, keeping at such a distance apart that we could see one another and everything between us; we walked the whole length of the wood up and then took the next section down, but slowly; for all the snow from the trees was now spread over the old snow on the ground; in some places it was packed down so hard that it bore our weight, but in other places we sank in to our knees. When we assembled the next time, in order to disperse anew, I inquired if after all it were likely that two small boys would have the courage to remain in the wood after it had grown dark. But this suggestion met with opposition from all. The boys were accustomed to be busied in the wood the whole day long and in the evenings too; they had other boys who constructed snow-men for them, forts and snow-houses, in which they often sat with lights, after it was dark.

This naturally drew our thoughts to all these buildings, and the possibility of the boys having taken refuge in one or other of them. But no one knew where they were situated this year, as the snow had come so recently.

Moreover, they were in the habit of building now in one place, now in another, and so nothing remained but to continue as before.

It so happened that Stina walked next to me this time, and as we two were in the ravine, and this was winding in some places, we were brought close together, and had no locality to search. She was evidently in a changed frame of mind. I asked her why this was.

" Oh," said she, " God has so plainly spoken to me. We are going to find the boys ! Now I know why all this has happened ! Oh, I know so plainly ! "

Her Madonna eyes glowed with a dreamy happiness; her pale, delicate face wore an expression of ecstasy.

" What is it, Stina ? "

" You were so hard toward me before. But I forgive you. Dear Lord, did not I sin myself? Did not I doubt God ? Did not I murmur against the decrees of God ? Oh, His ways are marvelous ! I see it so plainly — so plainly ! "

" But what do you mean ? "

" What do I mean ? Fru Atlung has for the last half year prayed God for only one single thing. Yes, it is her way to do so. She learned it of her father. Just for one single

thing she has prayed, and we have helped her.
It is that the boys may not be separated from
her; Atlung has threatened to send them away.
Had it not been for what has happened this
evening he would surely have kept his word;
but God has heard her prayer! Perhaps I too
have been an instrument in his hands; I almost
dare believe that I have. And the death of
little Hans, yes, most certainly the death of
little Hans! If those two sweet little souls
are sitting and freezing somewhere, waiting for
the angels, oh, the dear, dear boys, they surely
have these with them! Do you doubt this?
Ah, do not doubt! If the boys are made ill
— and they most surely will be ill — it will be
most fortunate for them! For when the father
and mother sit together beside the sick-bed, oh,
then the boys will never be sent away. Never,
no never! Then Atlung will see that it would
be the death of his wife. Oh, he sees it this
evening. Yes, he unquestionably sees it. He
has already made her a solemn promise; for the
last time we met, she gave me a look of such
heartfelt kindness, and that she did not do a
little while ago. It was as though she had
something to say to me — and what else could
it possibly be in the midst of her anxiety than
this? She has discerned God's ways, she too,

God's marvelous ways. She thanks and praises
Him, as I do ; yes, blessed be the name of God,
for Jesus Christ's sake, through all eternity!"

She spoke in a whisper, but decidedly, aye,
vehemently; the last, or words of thanksgiv-
ing, on the contrary, with bowed head, clasped
hands, and softly, as to her own soul.

We drifted apart, although now and then we
drew near together again, when the ravine
obliged us to do so, and all attempt at searching on our part ceased.

"There is one thing I need to have explained," I whispered to her. "If everything
from the time of the sorrowful death of little
Hans has happened in order that Atlung's
boys may remain with their mother; then
this great fall of snow we have recently seen
and heard must be part of the whole plan. But
I cannot see how?"

"That? Why that was simply a natural
occurrence; a pure accident."

"Is there such a thing?"

"Yes," replied she; "and it often has its
influence on the rest. To be sure, in this instance I cannot see how. It is a great mercy,
though, that I can see what I do. Why should
I ask more?"

We peered about us; but we felt convinced

that the boys were not in the ravine.   What I
had last said seemed to absorb Stina.

" What did *you* think about the snow-fall ? "
asked she, softly, the next time we were thrown
together.

" I will tell you.   Shortly before we came out
into the park, Fru Atlung had been saying to
me that the hope of immortality descended from
heaven on our lives, just as hushed, white, and
soft as the snow on the naked earth " —

" Oh, how beautiful ! " interposed Stina.

" And so I thought when the shock came,
and the whole forest trembled, and the snow
fell from the trees with the sound of thunder,
— now do not be angry, — that in the same
way the hope of immortality had fallen from
the mother of the boys, and you and all of us,
in our great anxiety for the lives of the little
fellows.   We rushed about in sorrow and lamentation, and some of us in ill-concealed frenzy,
lest the boys had received a call from the other
life, or lest some occurrence here had led them
to the brink of eternity."

" O my God, yes ! "

" Now we have had this hope of immortality
hanging over us for many thousand years, for
it is older, much older than Christianity ; and
we have progressed no farther than this."

"Oh, you are right! Yes, you are a thousand times right! Think of it!" she exclaimed, and walked on in silent brooding.

"You said before that I was hard toward you, and then I had done nothing but remind you of the belief in immortality you had taught the boys."

"Oh, that is true; forgive me! Oh, yes indeed!"

"For you know that you had taught them that it was far, far better to be with God than to be here; and that to have wings and be an angel was the highest glory a little child could attain; indeed, that the angels themselves came and carried away unhappy little children."

"Oh, I beg of you, no more!" she moaned, placing both hands on her ears. "Oh, how thoughtless I have been!" she added.

"Do not you believe all this yourself, then?"

"Yes, to be sure I believe it! There have been times in my life when such thoughts were my sole consolation. But you really confuse me altogether."

And then she told me in a most touching way that her head was no longer very strong; she had wept and suffered so much; but the hope of a better life after this had often been her one consolation.

Atlung's mournful call, with always the same words, was heard ever and anon, and just at this moment fell on our ears. With a start we were back again in the dreadful reality that the boys were not yet found, and that the longer the time that elapsed before they were found, the greater the certainty that they must pay the penalty of a dangerous illness. It continued to snow so that notwithstanding the moonlight we walked in a mist.

Then a cry rang through forest and snow from another voice than Atlung's and one of quite a different character. I could not distinguish what was said ; but it was followed by a fresh call from another, then again from a third, and this last time could be distinctly heard the words : " I hear them crying ! " It was a woman's voice. I hastened forward, the rest ran in front of and behind me, all in the direction whence came the call. We had become weary of wading in the heavy snow ; but now we sped onward as easily as though there were firm ground beneath our feet. The light from the lanterns skipping about among us and over our heads, shone in our eyes and dazzled us ; no one spoke, our breathing alone was heard.

" Hush ! " cried a young girl, suddenly halt-

ing, and the rest of us also stood still; for we
heard the voices of the two little ones uplifted
in that piteous wail of lamentation common to
children who have been weeping in vain for
long, long hours and to whom sympathy has
finally come.

"Good gracious!" exclaimed an elderly man,
— he well knew the sound of such weeping.
We perceived that the boys were no longer
alone; we walked onward, but more calmly.
We reached and passed the fish-pond, and came
to a place a little beyond the ravine, where the
trees were regular in their growth; for the
spot was sheltered and hidden. The weeping,
of course, became more distinct the nearer we
approached, and at last we heard voices blended
with it. They were those of the father and
mother, who had been the first to gain the spot.
When we had reached an opening where we
could see between the trees into the snow, our
gaze was met by two black objects against
something extremely white; it was the father
and mother, on their knees, each clinging to a
boy; behind them was a snow fort, or rather a
crushed snow house, in which, sure enough, the
boys had sought refuge. When the lanterns
were brought near, we saw how piteously benumbed with the cold the little fellows were:

they were blue, their fingers stiff, they could not stand well on their feet; neither of them had on caps; these no doubt lay in the heap of snow, if the boys had had them with them at all. They replied to none of the tokens of endearment or questions of their parents; not once did they utter a word, they only wept and wept. We stood around them, Stina sobbing aloud. The weeping of the boys, and the lamentations, questions, and tokens of endearment of the parents, together with the accents of despair and joy, which alternately blended therewith, were very affecting.

Atlung rose and took up one child; it was the elder one. His wife rose also, and gathered up the other in her arms. Several offered to carry the boy for her; but she made no reply, only walked on with him, consoling him, moaning over him, without a moment's pause between the words, until she made a misstep and plunging forward fell prostrate on the ground over her boy. She would not have help, but scrambled up with the boy still in her arms, walked on, and fell again.

Then she cast a look up to heaven, as though she would ask how this could happen, how it could be that this was possible!

Whenever I now recall her in her faith and

in her helplessness, I remember her thus, with
the boy in front of her stretched out in the
snow, and she bending over him on her knees,
tears streaming from the eyes which were uplifted with a questioning gaze toward heaven.

Some one picked up the boy, and Stina
helped his mother. But when the little fellow
found himself in the arms of another, he began
to cry: "Mamma, mamma!" and stretched
forth his benumbed hands toward her. She
wanted to go to him at once and take him again
in her arms, but he who carried the child hastened onward, pretending not to hear her, although she begged most humbly at last. They
had scarcely come down on the footpath before
she hastened forward and stopped the man ;
then with many loving words she took her boy
again in her arms. Atlung was no longer in
sight.

I allowed them all to go on in advance of
me.

But when I saw them a short distance from
me, enveloped in snow between the trees and
heard the weeping and the soothing words, I
drifted back into my old thoughts.

These two poor little boys had accepted literally the words of the grown people — to the
utter dismay of the latter ! If we were right

in our conjectures (for the boys themselves
had not yet told us anything and would not be
likely to tell anything until after the illness
they must unquestionably pass through) ; but
if we were right in our conjectures, then these
two little ones had sought a reality far greater
than ours.

They had believed in beings more loving than
those about us, in a life warmer and richer than
our own ; because of this belief they had braved
the cold, although amid tears and terror, waiting resolutely for the miracle. When the thunder rolled over them, they had doubtless trem-
blingly expected the change — and were only
buried.

How many had there been before them with
the same experience ?

CHAPTER VII.

I LEFT Skogstad at once, and without taking
leave of the parents, who were with their children. I got a horse to the next station, and
was soon slowly driving along the chaussée.
The snow which had fallen made the road

heavier than when I had come that way. A
few atoms still swept about through the air;
but the fall was lightening more and more, so
that the moonlight gradually gained in force.
It fell on the snow-clad forest, which still stood
unchanged, with fantastic power; for although
the details were lost the contrasts were striking.

I was weary, and the mood I was in har-
monized with my fatigue. In the still subdued moonlight the forest looked like a bowed-
down, conquered people; its burden was greater
than it could bear. Nevertheless, it stood there
patiently, tree after tree, without end, bowed to
the ground. It was like a people from the far-
distant past to the present day, a people buried in dust. Yonder "heaven-fallen, merciful
snow"—

And just as all symbols, even those from the
times of old, which mythology dimly reveals to
us, became fixed in the imagination, and gradually worked their way out to independence, so
it was now with mine. I saw the past generations enveloped in a cloud of dust, in which
they could not recognize one another, and that
was why they fought against one another, slay-
ing one another by the millions. Dust was
being continually strewed over them. But I
saw that it was the same with all those who

16

were wounded, or who must die. I saw in the
midst of these poor sufferers many kind, refined
souls, who in thus strewing dust were rendering
the highest, most beautiful service they knew,
like those priestly physicians of Egypt, who
offered to the sick and dying magic formulas
as the most effectual preventive of death, and
placed on the wounds a medicine, the greater
part of which was composed of mystic symbols.

And I saw *all* the relations of life, even the
soundest, strewed over with a coating of dust,
and the attempt at deliverance to be the world's
most complete revolution, which would wholly
shatter these relations themselves.

And as I grew more and more weary and
these fancies left me, but what I had recently
experienced kept rising uppermost in my mind,
then I plainly heard weeping in among the
snow-flakes that were no longer falling ; it was
the boys I heard. They wept so sorely, they
lamented so bitterly, while we tenderly bore
them from dust to more dust.

I passed through the forest and drove along
its margin up to the station. When I had
nearly reached this I cast one more look down-
ward over the tree-tops, which were radiant in
the moonlight. The forest was magnificent in
its snowy splendor.

The majesty of the view struck me now, and the symbol presented itself differently.

A dream hovering over all people, originating infinitely long before all history, continually assuming new forms, each of which denoted the downfall of an earlier one, and always in such a manner that the most recent form lay more lightly over the reality than those just preceding it, concealing less of it, affording freer breathing-space — until the last remnants should evaporate in the air. When shall *that* be ?

The infinite will always remain, the incomprehensible with it; but it will no longer stifle life. It will fill it with reverence; but not with dust.

I sat down in the sledge once more, and the monotonous jingle of the bells caused drowsiness to overcome me. And then the weeping of the boys began to ring in my ears together with the bells. And weary as I was I could not help thinking about what further must have happened to the two little fellows, and how it must appear at first in the sick-room at Skogstad, and in the surroundings of those I had just left.

How different was the scene I imagined from what actually occurred !

I could not but recall it when, two months

later, I drove over the same road with Atlung
and he related to me what had taken place. I
had then been abroad and he met me in town.

And when I now repeat this, it is not in his
words, for I should be totally unable to re-
produce them; but the substance of his story is
what follows.

The boys were attacked with fever, and this
passed into inflammation of the lungs. From the
outset every one saw that the illness must
take a serious turn; but the mother was so sure
that all had come to pass solely in order that
she might keep her boys, that she inspired
the rest of the household with her faith.

However serious the illness might be, it
would only be the precursor of happiness and
peace. While yet in the wood she had obtained
a solemn promise from her husband that their
children should not be sent away; but that
a tutor should be engaged for them who would
have them continually under his charge. And
by the sick-bed, when through the long nights
and silent days they met there, Atlung repeated this promise as often as his wife wished.
She had never been more beautiful, he had
never loved her more devotedly; she was in
one continual state of ecstasy. She confided
to Atlung that from the first time, about half

a year before, he had declared that the boys must go away, she had prayed the Lord to prevent it, prayed incessantly, and in all this time had prayed for nothing else. She knew that a prayer offered in the name of Jesus must be granted. She had prayed in this way several times before in regard to circumstances which seemed to herself to be brought into her life under the guidance of faith, brought into it in the most natural way. This time she had called her father to her aid and finally Stina; both of them had promised to pray only for this one thing. It did not seem to occur to her for a moment that there was another way of gaining her point, for instance, as far as lay within her power, and as far as her faith permitted it, to study Atlung's ideas on education, and to endeavor to persuade him to unite with her in an attempt, that it might be proved whether they were equal to the task. She started from the standpoint that she was utterly incompetent; what, indeed, was she able to do? But God could do what He would. This was his own cause, and that to a far higher degree than any other matter concerning which he had granted her prayers, and so she was sure He would hear her. Every occurrence, every individual who came to the gard, was sent; in one

way or another everything must be a link in the
chain of events, which was to lead Atlung to
other thoughts. When she told Atlung this, in
her innocence and her faith, he felt that, at all
events, there was no human power which could
resist her. He was so completely borne along
in the current of her fancies that he not only
became convinced that the boys would recover,
but he even failed to perceive how ill she was.

The long stay in the park, without any out-
door wraps and with wet feet, the overstrained
mental condition and long night vigils, the pursuit of one fixed idea, without any regard to its
effect on herself, being so wholly absorbed in it
that she forgot to eat, indeed, no longer felt the
need of food — wholly robbed her of strength
at last. But the first symptoms of illness were
closely united with her restless, ecstatic condition ; neither she herself, nor the rest of the
household paid any heed to them. When
finally she was obliged to go to bed, there still
hovered over her such joy, aye, and peace, that
the others had no time for anxiety. Her feverish fancies blended in such a way with her life,
her wishes, her faith, that it was often not well
to separate them. They all understood that
she was ill and that she was often delirious,
but not that she was in any danger. The phy-

sician was one of those who rarely express an opinion ; but they all thought that had there been danger he would have spoken. Stina, who had undertaken the supervision of the sick-room, was absorbed in her own fancies and hope, and explained away everything when At-lung showed any uneasiness.

Then one noon he came home from the fac-tories, and after warming himself, went up-stairs to the large chamber where the invalids all lay, for the mother wanted to be where the boys were. Her bed was so placed that she could see them both. Atlung softly entered the room. It was airy and pleasant there, and deep peace reigned. No one besides the in-valids, as far as he could see at first, was in the room ; but he afterwards discovered that the sick-nurse was there asleep in a large arm-chair, which she had drawn to the corner near-est the stove. He did not wake her ; he stood a little while bending over each of the boys, who were either sleeping or lying in a stupor, and thence he stepped very softly to his dear wife's bed, rejoicing in the thought that she too was now peaceful, perhaps sleeping ; for he did not hear her babble which usually greeted him. A screen had been placed between the bed and the window, so he could not see distinctly until

he came close to her. She lay with wide-open
eyes ; but tear after tear trickled down from
them.

" What is it ? " he whispered, startled. In
her changed mood he saw at once how worn,
how frightfully worn, she was. Why, in all
the world, had he not seen this before. Or had
he observed it, yet been so far governed by her
security that he had not .paid any attention
to it. For a moment it seemed as if he would
swoon away, and only the fear that he might
fall across her bed gave him strength to keep up.

As soon as he could he whispered anew,
" What is it, Amalie ? "

" I see by your looks that you know it yourself," she whispered slowly, in reply ; her lips
quivered, the tears filled her eyes and rolled
down her cheeks : but otherwise she lay quite
still. Her hands — oh, how thin they were ;
the ring was much too large on her finger, and
this he remembered having noticed before ; but
why had he not reflected on what it meant ?

Her hands lay stretched out on either side of
the body which seemed to him so slender beneath the coverlet and sheet. The lace about
her wrists was unrumpled, as though she had
not stirred since she was dressed for the morning, and that must now be several hours since.

" Why, Amalie," he burst out, and knelt down at her bedside.

" It was not thus I meant it," replied she, but in so soft a whisper that under other circumstances he could not have heard it.

" What do you mean by 'thus,' Amalie? Oh, try once more to answer me! Amalie!"

He saw that she wanted to reply, but either could not, or else had thought better of it. Tears filled her eyes and trickled down her cheeks, filled her eyes and were shed again, her lips quivered, but as noiselessly as this occurred, just so still she lay. Finally she raised her large eyes to his face. He bowed closer to her to catch the words: "I would not take them from — you," spoken in a whisper as before; the word "you" was uttered by itself, and in the same low tone as the rest, encompassed with a tenderness and a mournfulness which nothing on earth could exceed in strength.

He dared not question further, although he failed to understand his wife. He only comprehended that something had occurred that same forenoon which had turned the current of life to that of death. She lay there paralyzed. Her immobility was that of terror; something extraordinary had weighed her down to this speechless silence, had crushed her. But he

also comprehended that behind this noiseless
immobility there was an agitation so great that
her heart was ready to burst; he knew that
there was danger, that his presence increased
the danger, that there must be help sought; in
other words, he comprehended that if he did
not go away himself, his face as it must now
look was enough to kill her.   He never knew
how he got away.   He can remember that he
was on a stairway, for he recollects seeing a
picture that his wife herself must have hung up,
it was one representing St. Christopher carrying
the child Jesus over a brook.   He found himself lying on the sofa in the large sitting-room,
with something wet on his brow, and a couple
of people at his side, of whom one was Stina.
He struggled for a long time as with a bad
dream.   At the sight of Stina his terror returned.   " Stina, how is it with Amalie ? "
The answer was that she was in a raging fever.

" But what happened this forenoon while
I was absent ? "

Stina knew nothing.   She did not even understand his question.   She was not the one
who had attended Fru Atlung in the forenoon;
she had watched in the night, and then the
patient's fever fancies were happy ones, as they
had again become.   Had the doctor been with

her in the forenoon? No, he was expected now. He had said yesterday that to-day he would not come until later than usual. This indicated a feeling of security on the doctor's part.

Had Fru Atlung spoken with any one else? If so it must be the sick-nurse. "Bring her here!" Stina left the room. Atlung also sent away the others who had assembled around him, he needed to collect his thoughts. He sat up, with his head between his hands, and before he knew it he was weeping aloud. He heard his own sobs resounding through the large room and he shuddered. He felt sure; oh, he felt but too sure, that he would sit here alone and hear this wail of misery for weeks. And in this sense of boundless bereavement, her image stood forth distinctly: she came from her bed in her white garment and told him word for word what she had meant. Her prayer to God had been to be allowed to keep her boys, and now this had been granted in a terrible way for she was to have them with her in death. It was this which had paralyzed her. And the beloved one repeated: "I did not mean it thus, I would not take them from — you."

But how had this idea suddenly occurred to

her? *Why* was her security transformed into something so terrible?

The sick-nurse knew nothing. Toward morning the dear lady had fallen into a slumber, and this had gradually become more and more calm. When she awoke rather late in the morning, she lay still a little while before she was waited on. She was excessively weak; the housekeeper helped care for her. Not a word was said to her about her condition, not a single word. She had not spoken herself, except once; it was after she had had a little broth, then she said: " Oh, no, never mind ! " She lay back and closed her eyes. Her attendants urged her to take some more; but she made no reply. They stood a little and waited; then they left her in peace.

As the evening wore on, the fever increased ; by the doctor's advice she was carried into the next room. She understood this to mean that she was being borne into Paradise, and while they were moving her, she sang in a somewhat hoarse voice. She talked, too, now, without cessation ; but with the exception of that hymn about Paradise there was nothing in her words which indicated that she remembered anything that had occupied her thoughts in her moments of consciousness. All was now happiness and laughter once more. Toward morning she slept; but she woke very soon, and at once the unspeakable pain she had had before came over her, but at the same time came also the death-struggle. Amid this she became aware that the beds of the boys were not near hers. She looked at Atlung and opened her hand, as if she would clasp his. He understood that she thought the boys had gone on before and wanted to console him. With this cold little hand in his, and with its gentle pressure through the struggle with the last message from this receding life, he sat until the end came.

But then, too, he gave way wholly to his boundless grief. The responsibility he felt for not having attempted to draw her into his own vigorous reading and thought; for having left her to live a weak dream-life; to bear the burden of the housekeeping and the bringing up of the children, but not in community of spirit and will, partly out of consideration for her, partly from a careless desire to leave her as she was when he took her; for having amused himself with her when it struck his fancy to do so, but not having made an effort to work in the same direction with her, — this was what tormented his mind and could find no consolation, no answer, no forgiveness.

Not until the following night when he was wandering about out of doors, beneath a bright starlit sky, came the first soothing thoughts. Would she under any circumstances have forsaken the ideas of her childhood to follow his? Were not they an inheritance, so deeply rooted in her nature that an attempt to alter them would only have made her unhappy? This he had always believed, and it was this which ultimately determined him to live *his* life while she lived hers. The image of his beautiful darling hovered about him, and the two boys always accompanied her. Whether it was because of his own weariness, or whether his self-reproaches had exhausted themselves and let things speak their own natural language — his guilt toward her and toward them was shifted slightly and spread over many other matters, which were painful enough; but not as these were.

What these matters were, he did not tell me; but he looked ten years older than before.

The doctor sought an interview with him the next day, and said that he felt obliged to tell him that if he had not pronounced his wife's condition dangerous it was because he had felt sure that she would recover. Her own happy frame of mind would help her, he thought.

But something must have happened that fore-noon.

Atlung made no reply. The doctor then added that the boys were past all danger; the elder one, indeed, had never been in any.

Atlung had not yet for a moment separated mother and boys in his thoughts. During their illness he felt with her that they must live; for the last twenty-four hours he had been convinced that they must follow her in death. He could not think of the mother without them.

And now that he must separate them, the first feeling was — not one of joy: no, it was dismay that even in this matter the dear one had been disappointed! It seemed as though she were living and could see that it was all a mistake, and that this last mistake had needlessly killed her.

The two little boys, clad in mourning, were the first objects we met on the gard. They looked pale and frightened. They did not come to meet us, nor did they return their father's caress.

In the passage Stina met us; she too looked worn. I expressed my honest sympathy for her. She answered calmly that God's ways were inscrutable. He alone knew what was for our good.

Atlung took me with him to the family
burial-place, a little stone chapel in a grove
near the river. On the way there, he told me
that every time he tried to talk confidentially
with the boys and endeavor to be both father
and mother to them, his loss rushed over him
so overwhelmingly that he was forced to stop.
He would learn with time to do his duty.

The sepulchral chamber was a friendly little
chapel, in which the coffins stood on the floor.
The door, however, was not an ordinary door,
but an iron grating which now stood open ; for
there was work going on in the chapel. We
removed our hats, and walked forward to her
little coffin. We did not exchange a word.
Not until after we had left it and were looking
at the other coffins and their inscriptions, did
Atlung inform me that his wife's coffin was to
be placed in one of stone. I remarked that in
this way we would eventually have more of our
ancestors preserved than would be good for us.
" But there is reverence in it," he replied, as
we walked out.

There was warmth in the atmosphere. Over
the bluish snow, the forest rose green or dark
gray and the fjord was defiantly fresh. Spring
was in the air, although we were still in the
midst of winter.

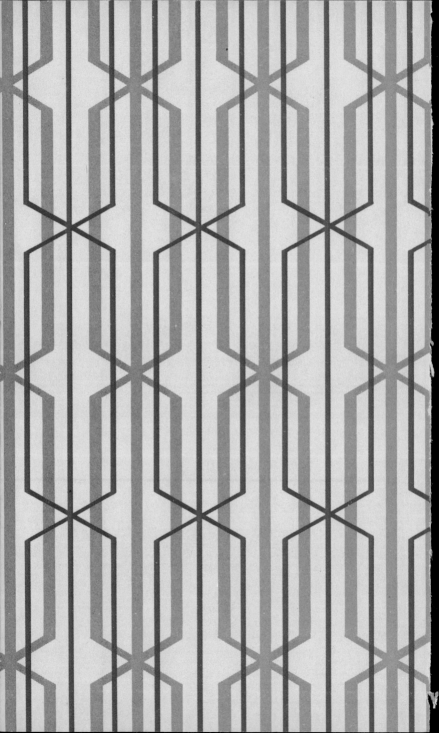